THE CASE OF NIKKI PAGAN

Rachel Eliason

ISBN: 978-0988573024

TOC

CHAPTER ONE

The Long Term Ward

JASON'S life had become alternating bands of light and dark. He felt hazy, drugged and disoriented. He ached all over but the pain was numbed and his mind too distant to focus on what hurt or why.

The helicopter was bright, harshly lit. A face floated over him. The nurse was male, adult but not old. He had wavy dark hair and a slender athletic build. He could have been Jason's older brother.

"Hang in there, buddy." He said, "we're coming in now."

There was the sound of activity all around him. The helicopter shuddered. A door opened.

People were moving around.

"It's going to be bumpy for a minute." The nurse warned and Jason's stretcher slid out into the night and darkness.

The light still burned a spot in the back of his retina. It shone like a bonfire, like the bonfire. Behind it the stars sparkled.

#

There was Dan, sitting beside Cynthia at the fire's edge. Jayden handing him a beer, Brittany taking it from him and forcing Jayden to hand over another. Her smug grin floated passed his face.

Ron's image was there too, holding up a can of Natural Light. "To 2013!" He roared at the night, "Our year to shine!"

Our year to shine, Jason thought dully.

#

There was a hiss of an automatic door and the lights of the ER hit him. New faces swam into his view; a doctor and for some reason his Aunt Mandy. What was she doing there?

"Mom and dad are on their way," she said to him as she patted his face. "They will be here in an hour or so."

An hour or so? He tried to shake his head but it was held immobile in a brace.

"You are on a spine board." Someone said in his ear, "until we can be sure there was no damage." He tried to nod to show he understood but the neck brace prevented movement in that direction too.

Mandy was talking to the doctor. She was saying something about his high school football team, how they had made it to state last year. Why was she telling the doctor about that? Surely there were more important things right now.

The doctor's answers were vague and mumbled. Jason tried to decipher them but could not. He caught "leg" "lots of damage" and "we'll do our best." Do their best what?

A bright light was shined in Jason's face and for a moment he saw double, like the headlights of a car.

#

A car.

"Are you okay to drive, bro?" Dan was saying as Jason stumbled out of Ron's parent's camper.

"Of course he is, silly," Brittany said as she stumbled into him. She was still pulling her shirt down, "Come on Jenny, Jenny." She called to her best friend Jenny Stevens. "We got to make curfew or my dad will kill me." Brittany and Jenny would slam an energy drink each on their way home and arrive sober enough to pass a cursory inspection and then pass out. Taking Jenny by the shoulder she led her away, towards Brittany's car.

"Don't worry so much, man." Ron said, "Jason's driven in a lot worse shape and been okay, right bro?"

Jason agreed, brushing off Dan's concern and stumbling towards his own car.

"See you Monday," Ron called as he turned away.

#

"Jason! Look at me," a voice commanded sternly and Jason pried his eyes open. "Follow the light." The voice commanded and Jason obeyed. "How many fingers am I holding up?"

"Two," Jason said groggily.

"Good, good," the voice went on. There were several more equally inane requests. He told them his full name. He said it was Thursday night, no, it Friday morning now, very early. No, he couldn't tell them the time.

"Where are you right now, Jason?"

"A hospital ER," He said. He tried to get his mind to work. He felt groggy, it was hard to focus He had come by helicopter. Mom and dad were an hour away. "Iowa City?"

"Good job," he was told, "good neuro signs," the voice said to someone else.

Then Jason was passing down a long hallway, lit at spaces by long fluorescent tubes. The lights flickered as he went passed, like the telephone poles on the dark road.

#

The telephone poles shone in his headlights like the gray ghosts of trees. He blinked and felt the car starting to drift on the gravel. His eyes snapped open and he righted the car again.

Driving alone down the dark gravel road Jason's head began to bob again. He fought to stay awake. Slam an energy drink, he told himself, act sober for a couple of minutes when you walk in the door. That was a good idea. He had one too, in the glove box. He reached for it, fought the latch on the glove box and pulled his eyes off the road for a split second.

Bang.

#

Jason jolted awake.

"Just transferring you onto the CAT scan," a voice said, "It's going to be okay."

Another voice, a woman this time, said, "We need you to lay very still now, for quite a while. We're going to give you something to help you keep still, okay?"

#

Jason sat in his car, disoriented. Blood ran from his head but it seemed to be running up, not down. He was dizzy. He couldn't figure out why the blood was running up. He tried to move but a sudden sharp pain along his right side stopped him. His leg was trapped holding him in place, crushed between the collapsed steering column and some nameless metal part that had been driven through the engine. In the remains of his windshield all he could see was dirt. Through the driver's side window was a haze of dust and the beams of his car's headlights.

#

When Jason woke again he was back in the ER. The drugged feeling was wearing off. His entire right leg felt like it was on fire. He shifted his weight and found the neck and back brace were gone. He managed to move only a fraction of an inch, the pain that shot through him was unbearable. He winced and let out a groan.

"Don't try to move, hon," His mom's voice said. Her face appeared at his bedside. "Markus," she said calling his father, "go tell that nurse I think his pain medication is wearing off."

"I am here." A voice said before his father could reply, "Perfect timing too. We've got a suite prepared in OR. I've got his pre-anesthetic with me."

"What's going on mom?" Jason asked.

His dad's face appeared at his bedside next to his mom. "You're going to surgery," his dad answered "they're going to try to save your leg. We will be there when you get out, I promise."

"Try?" He whispered as the world began to fade to black once more.

#

The short term pediatric ward has it's seasonal rhythm, they see a spike of accidents during the summer when children and young adults are out being active and a spike of respiratory ailments in the fall and winter. The long term pediatric ward was another sort of beast all together, with rhythms no doctor or nurse had yet penetrated.

The damage to Jason's leg was such that there was no doubt he would have to stay a long time. Not wanting him exposed to constant traffic and potential sources of infection, his surgeon would not allow him on the high traffic short term ward. Due to circumstances no one could expect or control there was only one bed left on the long term ward, in a double room. The problem of a roommate seemed on the verge of correcting itself. The boy's family walked hurriedly and quietly past Jason's bed and disappeared behind the curtain. They spoke softly to each other from time to time. His mom had whispered to him that the boy had cancer and was dying.

Jason caught a brief glimpse of his roommate when one of the nurses pulled the curtain after doing something with him. He looked the part of the cancer boy to a T. He had pale light skin and was skinny and bald. His pale blues eyes took Jason in with a lethargic look before the nurse pulled the curtain again.

The quiet was infectious. Jason and his parents conversed in whispers too. They told him the surgery went as well as could be expected. His shinbone had been shattered, an artery had been severed at knee level and his upper thigh had significant "soft tissue damage" whatever that meant.

Still they had saved his leg. They had replaced a portion of the artery with an artificial graft and his lower leg now contained "hardware". It was going to be a long road to recovery, his dad said, but he was going to make it.

His entire right side felt battered and bruised. His right leg was a numb, dull ache that would not go away. He couldn't move it all. Even attempting, even tensing the muscles on that side sent shivers of pain through his body. The nurses brought syringes of something for his IV, Morphine he assumed, at regular intervals and it made the pain bearable. It did nothing for the moments of near panic when he allowed his mind to wonder just how bad the leg was and whether or not he would ever walk again.

#

When Jason woke it was late afternoon. The afternoon sun spread across the floor at the foot of his bed. His family was gone. The other kid's family was gone too, and the curtain pulled back. The boy lay still and Jason assumed, hoped, he was sleeping. Surely they wouldn't leave him alone with a dead body?

There was a clatter at the door. The sound must have been what had woke him. He watched through slitted eyes as a wheelchair made its slow awkward progress into the room.

The only adjective that Jason could find for the person navigating the chair was interesting. She, though he was only half certain it was a girl, had brownish red hair that was a couple inches shy of shoulder length, as though she had just began growing it out. Her face was narrow and pinched, her nose long but not unattractive. She looked to be a year or two younger than Jason's seventeen but clearly a teen. Her brown eyes were intent on her navigation and she did not greet him. He kept his eyes slits and did not acknowledge that he had noticed her either.

There was no IV bag hanging from her wheelchair. He did notice as she broke free from the end of his bed that there was a catheter bag hanging underneath the wheelchair.

She rolled across the room to the boy's bed. She came to a stop alongside the bed and leaned way over in her chair so she was hanging over his bed rail. Jason found himself staring at her chest, trying to decipher if she were a small chested girl or in fact a boy.

She reached over and poked the dying boy none too gently in the chest, "You dead?" She asked.

His eyes opened and regarded her wearily, but a sly smile played across his lips, giving his face more animation that Jason had yet seen there. "No," he answered quietly, "not yet."

"Want some pudding then?" She prompted.

He shrugged. "Sure."

She rescued something from her lap. "Vanilla or Chocolate?" She asked holding up two pudding cups.

"Vanilla," he replied.

She handed over a pudding cup and plastic spoon. Then she turned her head and favored Jason with a smile. "I've an extra chocolate if you're interested?"

Lunch had been soft foods, pudding, apple sauce and Jello mostly. They promised with supper his diet would be "advanced" whatever that meant. His stomach lurched and he nodded, "sure, thanks."

"It's okay, I got a source." She said. She maneuvered her wheelchair away from the boy's bed and rolled over to Jason. "I'm Nikki, you've met Bobby I assume."

"Actually, we haven't." Bobby said. He gave Jason a wave. "Hi, I am Bobby." He said.

"My name's Jason," Jason supplied.

Nikki had a box of chocolate pudding cups, an empty box of vanilla and a small collection of plastic spoons. She handed him a cup and a spoon. "So I take it you're in for your leg?"

In for? He chuckled to himself. *Was this prison?* "What makes you say that?" He asked casually.

"Well, there's a piece of metal sticking out of it for one." She replied in a matter of fact tone. She rolled her chair back against the wall so she could face both boys without blocking their view of each other.

Jason craned his head to see his right leg. She was right. He had not one, but two pieces of metal sticking out of his leg, the first just below the knee and the second just above the ankle. A third metal bar ran from one to the other. *Hardware indeed.* A quick peek under the covers informed him that the metal went all the way through his leg and out the other side. There was a cross piece on that side as well. Also, he was not wearing underwear at the moment. He pulled the covers back down embarrassed. He glanced sheepishly at Nikki but she didn't seem to have noticed his nakedness. "Damn, I didn't realize." He said.

"You didn't know you had pieces of metal sticking out your leg?" Bobby asked.

"I've been pretty drugged up since the accident," Jason said embarrassed.

"What kind of accident?" Nikki asked.

"My car," he started and stopped. "Umm, I crashed it pretty bad."

"Yeah," Bobby agreed, "I heard your parents talking to mine earlier, sounds like you nearly lost your leg."

"So is it true?" Nikki asked. Jason looked at her and then realized she wasn't talking to him. He followed her gaze to Bobby. "Are you dying?" She finished.

Bobby gave a resigned shrug. "I've felt like crap since yesterday," he said, "and I've got no energy. They don't know what's wrong, though. My cancer doc suggested a full body cat scan, again." He rolled his eyes. "God only knows what that will show."

"What?" Jason started then stopped, not knowing quite what to ask or how.

"Sarcoma." Bobby said, "Rapid growing Aleveor Sarcoma, to be exact. It's a rare form of cancer. Tumors appear in soft tissue."

Soft tissue? The doctor had said something about Jason having "soft tissue" damage.

"What's soft tissue mean?" He asked.

Bobby laughed ruefully, "basically anything that ain't bone. Mine is metastatic. That means the cancer has gotten everywhere. You wouldn't believe where some of the tumors have popped up. It's pretty gross really."

"Can they cure it?" Jason asked.

Bobby shrugged again.

"They can try," Nikki said, "they won't ever stop trying, not on someone our age."

"The chemo has slowed it, kept me mostly out of the hospital for the better part of a year, but new growths keeping popping up and the prognosis keeps getting worse." Bobby said. "They had to surgically remove one from my midsection about a month ago and I've been here ever since. Luckily, Nikki showed up a couple of weeks later to keep me company."

"Yup," Nikki agreed, "that's exactly why I am here. Say did you here," Nikki began talking about another patient, an eight year old with cancer that both of them knew. Jason ate his pudding in silence. He couldn't follow much of the conversation because he didn't know any of the same people but it was nice to listen. After the hushed dread of the morning's conversation this ordinary conversation was comforting somehow.

After some time a middle aged female nurse with long dark hair held back in a pony tail stuck her head in the room. "I figured I'd find you here." She said to Nikki. "A doctor is waiting for you."

Nikki gave her a resentful look but nodded. "I've got to go," she said. She gave Bobby a wistful look, "I hope you don't die yet."

"Thanks for the pudding cup." Jason said as Nikki maneuvered herself out the door. It was a stupid thing to say, especially compared to "I hope you don't die" but somehow he felt like he should acknowledge her departure somehow.

#

Before coming to the long term pediatric ward Jason had been blissfully unaware that a smell could be so bad that it would wake you from a dead sleep. Yet he was woken that night by a smell almost as foul as it was unidentifiable. It made what little supper he had been allowed roll unpleasantly in his stomach. The smell he decided was somewhere between a porta potty left in the heat too long and meat that had went bad. He left it at that, feeling it was perhaps best not to more fully identify what it was.

There was a noise too, but it was less demanding of attention. It was a high pitched electronic noise, a persistent "bing, bing, bing". There was light, coming out of the bathroom door. Other more human noises were coming from that direction as well. Jason shifted his weight and looked over at Bobby. The bed was empty.

Footsteps approached. "What's," a female voice said at the bathroom door and then, "oh my."

More footsteps approached. A male aide entered the room and pulled a wheelchair out from the far side of the bed. He rolled it to the bathroom. There were others arriving, three or four in all. Bobby looked even more pale and weak as they wheeled him back towards the bed, one nurse pushing the wheelchair and another pulling the IV pole.

He gave Jason a resigned look of apology as they helped him into bed. The nurse had a cellphone out and was talking as she left the room, "Yes, doctor Lin? Sorry to disturb you but," and then she was gone.

The male aid returned shortly with a bottle of air freshener. The vaguely pine/chemical odor did little to mask the other smell. The second nurse, his nurse, returned as well. "I see you're awake. Do you need something for pain?"

He grimaced at the reminder and nodded yes.

CHAPTER TWO

Today is Not a Good Day to Die

IT was light when Jason woke. Bobby was sitting up, his feet dangling off the side of his bed. He was wearing hospital scrubs and a blue stocking cap. He was playing on a Nintendo DS. He looked pale in the light of day, but more energetic then Jason had seen him yet.

Jason coughed and moved in the bed. Bobby looked up and smiled. "Well I'm not dying, bro," he said. "At least not right now." He pulled the cap down and set down the DS. "Sorry about last night. God, just when you think your life can't get any grosser."

"What happened?"

"I was shitting blood." Bobby answered wryly. "I guess one of the tumors in my gut broke loose or something. Anyway," he gestured at his IV, which was now red, "they've been giving me blood all night and I feel a ton better. Must have been what was making me feel like crap."

"My god, I'm sorry," Jason said.

"Hey, at least I don't have a piece of metal sticking out of my leg," Bobby said sardonically.

Jason started to get mad but stopped himself from responding. After all the kid was dying of cancer.

"That's the thing about this place," Bobby went on with a thin smile, "no matter how bad you've got it somebody else got a piece of metal sticking out of their leg or," he broke off. "Something worse. There's a kid down the hall with a spinal injury that is on a ventilator, and will be for life. I'd offer to introduce you but he's got some weird infection on top of everything else so none of us are allowed to see him anymore."

"I am glad you aren't dying," Jason said.

"Why not? You'd get the room to yourself." Bobby answered.

Jason didn't know how to answer. Nobody taught you how to feel or act around someone like Bobby, someone who was dying of cancer. "I wish there was something I could do," he said.

Bobby seemed to sense Jason's

discomfort. "There's nothing anyone can do." He said. He paused for a long while and then added, "you know why I like Nikki so much? She talks to me like a normal person. Most people are too uncomfortable to even visit me, and those that do talk in whispers. The worse it is, the quieter they talk."

He stood suddenly. He pulled a can of Axe deodorant spray from his bedside table. Pulling the IV pole alongside him, he handed the can to Jason. "Take this, you're going to need it in a minute." He headed for the bathroom.

#

"Hey Jason, my name is Alex and I am going to be your primary nurse," the man said from the foot of Jason's bed. He had short sandy blond hair and pale green eyes. Alex looked to be a couple of inches shorter than Jason but broader. He looked like he worked out, a lot.

"Okay," Jason said.

Alex quickly introduced the two nurse with him as Jenny and Lynn. All three had their hands full and Jason couldn't help but wonder who and what all those medical supplies were for.

"Umm, so what's a primary nurse?" He asked.

"That means every day that I am here, I will be assigned to your case. We will get to know each other, but more importantly I will get to know all your doctors, what they want for your care, what appointments and test you have, that sort of thing. I am sort of the go-to-guy on your case." Alex explained.

"How many doctors do I have?" Jason said.

Alex thought a moment, "Right now, four." He said.

"Lightweight," Bobby joked from the far side of the curtain.

"Dr. Faye was the trauma doc when you came in and is still technically in charge of your case, but I doubt she will stay on. Dr. Jensen was the ortho doc that did the lower leg surgery. He'll be your primary doc. Dr. Shadur was the vascular surgeon that did the vein graft. He had some helpers, residents, but they won't be following. Finally, Dr. Jan is the rehab specialist who will be seeing you about physical therapy for your leg. Dr. Heimdall is the infectious disease doctor." Alex said.

Jason was quickly lost in the maze of names and titles he didn't understand. "Infectious?" Jason asked, "I don't have a disease, do I?"

"No, no," Alex assured him. "The wound nurses answer to him, so he's on your case."

"Wound nurses?" Jason said. It dawned on him suddenly who all the supplies were for.

"Yup," Alex said, "They got a look at your wound the yesterday while you were still pretty much out of it. They've left detailed instructions, starting this morning, for dressing changes."

"What are you going to do?" Jason asked

nervously.

"First thing," Alex answered, "is a shot of morphine. This might hurt. After today they'll be starting to switch you to pills instead of shots, and you'll know if this is going to hurt really bad or not. So in the future I will check with you beforehand and see if you need something or not. For today it's better safe than sorry.

Jason's mother made her entrance while Alex was slowly injecting the drug into Jason's IV. Alex explained to his mother how they were about to do the dressing change. It was something he called a "wet to dry" dressing. Jason had stopped even trying to figure out all the new terms that were being thrown at him.

While Alex talked, the other two nurses lifted and held Jason's leg. It was awkward and uncomfortable but not nearly as painful as he had feared it would be. Alex donned gloves and began to unravel the brown dressing around Jason's leg. There was a another layer of white cotton dressings underneath that and Alex cut that away with a pair of scissors. Finally Jason's bare leg was exposed.

He stared at in horror for one second and then looked away. "Mom!" He said in a frightened voice. "Mom, my leg!"

His mom bent over his face, taking his hands, "It's okay honey, It's okay." She said soothingly but her face looked pale too.

"What the hell Mom?" Jason went on, not particular soothed, "There, there," he almost couldn't bring himself to say it. "There are chunks missing, Mom!"

"Jason," Alex said firmly, "Chill. I know it's hard, but you're gonna get through this, I promise."

He looked back at Alex's face. It was impassive and cool. It might have helped Jason calm down except his eyes wanted to wander down to his leg again. His right thigh had a strip running down it, starting about midthigh that had essentially no skin. The strip was maybe three inches wide. He could see the underlying flesh, beefy red, clearly. Worse still there were two small mounds of gauze, mounds that Alex was removing to reveal two deep gouge marks into the muscle. He snapped his eyes forward, focusing on his mother's face instead. "What the heck happened?" He asked.

"You bounced off a concrete culvert," Alex said. "It drove the gear box up, then you slammed the far side of the ditch and it drove the steering wheel down and crushed your leg between them. They had to use the jaws of life to pull them apart. It did a lot of damage to your leg. The good news is that it held you pretty still, which is probably why you don't have a head injury as well."

Jason fought to master his breathing. He wanted to scream. How could Alex mention good news while a big chunk of Jason's leg was gone? His mom at least seemed to understand his anxiety. She held his hand and ran her fingers through his hair while he stared resolutely at the wall.

Alex went on talking about the accident and explaining what he was doing. Jason tuned him out and the nurse's voice became little more than a calming drone behind him. A drone that helped him not think about the fact that they were currently packing gauze soaked in some vinegar smelling solution into what remained of his leg.

The dressing change lasted only ten minutes or so, but it felt much longer. The sense of just how bad his accident had been lingered throughout the day. It was accented by a steady stream of visitors and well-wishers, and by Bobby's adage, "the worse it is, the quieter they talk."

Jason's dad showed up shortly after they had finished re-wrapping the leg. He asked Jason how he was doing. Jason wanted to tell him about the leg but couldn't find the words. Finally he gave up and said "okay I guess, considering." His father nodded and didn't pry.

His mom mentioned that they had done a dressing change on the leg but she too shied away from trying to describe the mess that was his leg. The two talked in a hushed whisper about nothing. Finally they excused themselves to go to the cafeteria and then back to the hotel dad had gotten for the weekend. It had been a long night for both of them.

A man dressed in hospital scrubs arrived

with a cart minutes after they left. He said, "Bobby?" in an uncertain voice. Bobby waved and the man introduced himself as a "transporter." Bobby nodded wearily and stood. He pulled his IV pole over and sat on the cart. The man removed the bag and hung it from another pole that was attached to his cart. Bobby lay back patiently while the man worked.

Jason's coach, Mr. Terrance showed up just as they were rolling Bobby out. "The full body cat scan they promised," He groused with a goodbye wave to Jason, "Even though I am feeling better."

"Good luck," Jason called after him. To his coach he added a guilty, "Sorry Mr. Terrance I don't think I am going to be able to do that summer workout routine you planned."

"It's okay son, we are all just glad you're alive." That was it. Nothing about "get better by the fall season". Coach Terrance repeated the "glad you're alive" phrase several times but he never mentioned Jason's recovery prospects and he never asked a single question about the accident. He didn't seem to know what to talk about. He excused himself after just ten minutes, saying that he and his wife were going shopping in Coralville before heading out of town. He shook Jason's hand and said again, "I am glad you're alive."

Less than a half an hour later a couple of Mom and Dad's friends showed up. They didn't stay much longer than the coach and had nothing more substantial to say.

Aunt Mandy came mid morning. She had his mom with her. They sat with him for a half hour or so and then went to the gift shop for a while.

Jenny came with her mother, a nurse, for a short visit. Jason was pretty sure it was her mother's idea. He wondered sourly why Brittany, his girlfriend, wasn't rushing to his side. But they weren't really that close and he knew that hospitals freaked her out.

That afternoon it was a couple of guys from the team. They were the first people his age that had made the two hour trip by themselves. They had a card that they had gotten signed by most of the team and quite a few of the other students from school, especially considering it was summer.

Mostly though it was adults, friends of Jason's mom and dad. They brought cards. No one seemed to know exactly what to say and they all seemed very uncomfortable. It was the same hushed voices that Bobby's family had used the day before.

The steady stream of visitors did little to help Jason's mood. The morphine made him groggy and drunk feeling. The feeling, coupled with the fact that not one person asked him directly about his accident, made him feel increasingly guilty as the day progressed. Did they know he had been drunk when he crashed his car? He wasn't sure and he wasn't sure how to ask either.

When Bobby was brought back in the late afternoon, Jason was glad to see him. He felt like he understood, no matter how distantly, what Bobby had gone through. One day of people whispering, one day of no one wanting to talk normally to him, made Jason feel a bond with Bobby.

Bobby however was in a foul mood. The initial results of his CAT Scan were inconclusive, he said. "All that for basically nothing," he complained bitterly.

A few minutes later Nikki made her entrance. She was pushed in by a younger nurse with shoulder length blond hair.

"We've got one of the good nurses," Nikki said, introducing the nurse as "Angie". The nurse gave a slightly conflicted frown at being described as "one of the good nurses".

"What does that mean?" Jason asked.

"It means she can stay longer," Bobby said, brightening slightly.

"And ice cream," Nikki added.

"Chocolate, Vanilla, or Orange Sherbet?" The nurse asked recovering quickly.

"Ooh, sherbet," Bobby said.

"Me, too," Jason put in.

Nikki cocked her eye at Jason. "Okay the cancer boy I understand, touchy stomach and all, but you?"

"I love sherbet." Jason protested, "always have."

She said indignantly, "how can anyone turn down chocolate?"

Jason smiled and almost laughed, not because it was particularly funny but because after an entire morning of hushed conversations about his leg being teased about his ice cream preferences felt so normal. If there was one thing he needed right now, it was for something to seem normal.

"I'm with you," Angie said to Nikki. "But to each his own. One chocolate and two sherbets coming up."

She disappeared and reappeared promptly with ice cream cups and spoons. Nikki once again backed her chair against the wall so they could all converse with the minimal of head turning.

They talked about the most inane of things, but it felt good. Nikki groused about the poor selection of young adult books in the hospital library, and her parents lived almost three hours away. They would come about once a week or so is all. They would bring a book or two but Nikki would breeze through that in a couple of days.

"My aunt Mandy lives in town," Jason said, "I can ask her to pick up some books from the town library, I am sure they have lots. What kind of books do you read?"

"Anything supernatural," she said.

"Harry Potter sort of stuff?"

"Read it," she said, "and Twilight and all those. I like most werewolf sort of books, or fay."

"Fay?"

"Faeries," she said, "but not little flower fairy sorts of books, or folklore, I like novels about magical beings that come to this world."

"I didn't even know they had those," Jason said.

"Just wait," Nikki told him, "spend a couple of weeks in this place, let alone a couple of months, and you'll know everything there is to know about books and old movies."

"And video games, and surfing the internet." Bobby said, "not much else to do when you lay around all day."

Jason grimaced. "I have no idea how long I am even in for."

"Is it bad?" Nikki asked.

"I have a chunk out of my leg." Jason said. It was the first he had talked about it since the morning.

"A chunk?" Nikki said amazed.

"My god!" Bobby added. "I'm sorry I joked about it earlier."

"Its okay," Jason told him. It felt good to say it out loud, but he didn't really want to talk about it too much so he changed the subject again, "So books about magical beings, I'll ask her the next time she stops by. Or maybe I'll call her tonight, so she can bring them next time."

"That would be great," Nikki said.

"And she really likes," Bobby started but Nikki burst in,

"Don't you dare, Bobby McGin! I know stuff about you too!"

"I had this laptop for a while. It got a virus and got fried but I used to loan it to Nikki from time to time." He started to explain with a smile on his face.

Nikki started her wheelchair towards his bed threateningly, though she too had a smile on her face. "I'm warning you." She said.

"So I borrowed her my laptop for a couple of days and it came back with a bunch of fan fic on it."

"Fan fic?"

"You know where fan's write their own stories based on the characters. Like where they take characters from Harry Potter or Twilight but then write their own stories." Bobby explained. With a final sly look he said, "even erotic stories."

Nikki spun on Jason, "just wait until Tuesday, man. That boy hasn't missed an episode of Glee since he got sick." She said.

"I made peace with being a geek a long time ago," Bobby said smugly.

They were still arguing about whose secret was worse when the evening nurse stuck her head in and told Nikki she had to return to her own room for supper.

Jason's mood was temporarily lifted by the visit. When his evening nurse, a mousy woman whose name he promptly forgot, offered him pain pills instead of the shot he assumed that it meant he was getting better. His mood fell again when she told him he would have to go through the whole dressing change again, in fact they would do it twice a day for the foreseeable future.

CHAPTER THREE

The Mystery of Nikki

THE next morning it was Jason's turn to be hauled away for tests. His nurse, it was Alex's day off, told him about the tests when she did the morning dressing change. He didn't understand even one tenth of what she said but it was better than thinking about what she was doing to his leg. What he understood was that they wanted to test the blood flow in his leg, especially beneath the artery graft. They would have to inject some sort of chemical into his veins and then do a Cat Scan. He would be gone a good stretch of the morning, but hopefully not all day.

Less than a half an hour later the

transporter person arrived. The guy pushed the call light and when the secretary (or whoever it was that answered the intercom) answered he asked for lifting help.

About a half dozen people answered the call. It was soon apparent that they would all be needed. A running back, Jason weighed about 200 pounds in season, most of it muscle. Off season he was a little heavier. But it wasn't just his weight. He couldn't move his leg at all on his own. With the metal pins and the wound it took a couple of people just lift and move his leg.

The middle aged nurse from the first day made an appearance after they had gotten Jason on the stretcher. Nikki had called her Andrea and another less flattering name. "I figured while we had everyone together," she said and made a gesture with her head.

The crowd followed her out of his room. He glanced over at Bobby, but the curtain was drawn.

As Jason rolled out into the hall he saw the crowd was hanging out. Nikki was coming out of her room, a determined look on her face.

"It's time, Nikki," the nurse said.

"I was just going to the lounge for a while, come back later." She replied. Her voice had a tinny sound to it, like she was trying to be casual but failing.

"Come on," one of the male aides said softly, "let's just get this over with and then you can go to the lounge if you want."

Just outside her door one of the nurses caught the handle of her wheelchair, stopping her forward progress.

The transporter stuck Jason's medical chart under his pillow and began to roll the stretcher down the hall. Jason twisted his head frantically, trying to catch the action.

"Nikki," Andrea was saying, "We've got to do this."

"No! You don't!" Nikki was insisting, "just cuz the doctor said, don't mean you have to. You've said no to him on other things, I've heard."

With that Jason's stretcher turned the corner. The last image he had was of Nikki rolling backward into her room, a half dozen staff slowly filtering in after.

"What was that all about?" He asked the transporter, who merely shrugged.

Nikki's face haunted him throughout the test. He couldn't shake it. Her mouth set in determination but fear in her eyes. What were they doing to her?

#

When they wheeled him back to the unit everything was quiet. Nikki's door was closed and he had no clue if she was inside or not. The same gang of nurses appeared to help him back into his bed. After they had him situated they left, leaving him alone with his nurse.

"Are you ready for lunch?" She asked, "do you need a pain pill?"

Jason's leg ached from being moved about. He nodded yes. As the nurse was leaving he called her back, "nurse?"

"Yes?"

"This morning when I was leaving, what was going on?"

The nurse stiffened. "You mean across the hall?" She asked suspiciously.

He nodded.

"I can't talk about other patients, Jason." She said flatly.

"I just want to know is she okay?"

The nurse scowled and didn't answer. Then finally she repeated, "we are not allowed to talk about any patient under our care. It's confidentiality. I can assure you we treat anything you tell us with the same respect."

"I don't care what you tell her!" He said angrily. Then he stopped. He did care. If they knew he was drunk at the time of the accident, he certainly didn't want Nikki to know that.

He started to try again but the nurse had already left. He promised himself that he would ask again and again until he knew Nikki was okay.

Just then Brittany walked in. For the longest time she just stood there, looking at him.

"You can come in," he said. "It's okay."

She came to his left side, away from the damage. She leaned in and gave him a short peck on the cheek. "I'm sorry." She said.

She didn't sound very sorry. She sounded

more put out that she had to come all the way to Iowa City and brave a hospital because he had the gall to wreck his car and get himself injured.

"How is it?" She asked after an almost painfully long pause.

He looked at his leg, covered by a sheet, and considered his answer. "Not too good," he said finally, "but they saved the leg. I guess that's something."

She swore softly.

"How have you been?" He asked.

"A mess since they told me." She said. She didn't look like she had been a mess, but Jason didn't know what he expected. Actually, he did know what he expected but Brittany wasn't the type to come running into the ER, mascara running from the tears.

"Mom drove me up," Brittany volunteered after some time.

"That was nice of her but why?" Jason said. Brittany had driven herself and her friends to go shopping in Iowa City multiple times before.

"I am not allowed to drive," she said sullenly. "I was still pretty drunk when they woke me to tell me about your accident."

Part of Jason could feel sympathy for Brittany. He could just imagine the sort of trouble she was in. Nor was she likely alone. How many kids had been at the party? How many were sober enough to pass when their parents woke them?

Another part of him was furious, a bitter cold sort of anger. It didn't matter how long she was grounded for, even if it was all summer. He had pieces of metal holding his leg in place so it could heal. He had a chunk of his thigh missing. They had barely saved his leg. Nobody had yet told him, and he was terrified to ask, if he would ever be able to walk again. So what if she got grounded? So what if she had to visit a hospital? He was stuck here for god knows how long.

She must have sensed his anger because she spoke no more about her confinement or the party. She tried a couple of times to tell him some gossip about the kids back home but when he gave no more than mono syllabic responses she gave up.

After the longest half hour he had ever endured she decided she had stayed long enough. She rose, gave him a second quick peck on the cheek and left saying she'd come back when she could.

His mom and Aunt Mandy came around four that afternoon, which was good because Jason was bored stiff. Bobby was gone with his mother and Jason had spent the last three hours flipping channels more or less at random, unable to focus on anything for longer than a few minutes.

They brought pizza and asked him about his day. He didn't have much to tell them. He told them about his test that morning, but he didn't know the results yet. The radiologist lady had given him a thumbs up as they wheeled him out so he assumed it was good news.

He made the mistake of mentioning that Brittany had stopped by. They both treated this as great news and he quickly changed the subject because he didn't want to discuss how it had made him feel. He was starting to question his own reaction. Surely she was just really upset about things? He shouldn't misjudge her by thinking she was more put out by the inconvenience of his accident.

Then he thought about the incident that morning. He didn't want to discuss that either but it reminded him to ask Aunt Mandy to bring Nikki some library books.

"What about you? Is there anything you want?" His mom asked.

Jason shrugged. He had never been much of a reader. "I suppose it wouldn't hurt, though I don't know what book. Maybe you could bring my iPad next time, so I can get online. Also Bobby's got an Xbox. He says it would be cool if someone brought some of my games."

"Bobby?" His mom asked.

"My roommie," he explained nodding at the other bed.

His mom's voice dropped, "the boy who's dying?"

The tone bothered him. "He's rallied or something," he said irritably. "Anyway his name is Bobby and he's cool."

"Hear that mom?" Bobby's voice came from the doorway, "I am officially cool."

He rolled in, being pushed by his mother. He was wearing a University of Iowa shirt, blue sweat pants and the same blue stocking cap he had worn that morning. His mom parked the wheelchair a few feet from the bed and Bobby stood up, looking pretty strong. He sat on the side of his bed and patted the spot next to him. His mom sat.

They talked for a long time. Mrs. McGin had been bringing Bobby to the University Hospitals and Clinics for a couple of years now, including one other long stay in the hospital. She was knowledgeable about the hospital and the local area. She gave Jason's mom plenty of advice from the best vending machine locations to who to talk to when the medical bills started rolling in. Jason felt another pang of guilt at the thought of how much this was going to cost his mom and dad.

"Want to watch something?" Bobby asked after the women had left for the night.

"Naw," Jason answered, "I am beat. I think I am going to pass out."

"Me too," Bobby agreed, "that outing took a lot out of me." Then he laughed dryly, "we are pathetic, you know that. Who would have thought, a couple of teenagers turning in before nine pm."

Jason laughed too. "Yeah, who'd think a little thing like cancer or a messed up leg would stop the party."

Jason lay there for a long time, tired but unable to sleep. After a long time he said, "hey

Bobby, you still awake?"

"Hmm?" Bobby answered sleepily.

"Bobby, is someone crying?"

The soft noise continued. Bobby took so long in answering that Jason thought he'd fallen back asleep and was startled when he finally answered. "Yeah, sounds like Nikki."

"This morning something happened," he started and paused, not sure how to continue. He didn't have to.

"Damn," Bobby said quietly, "I had forgotten, it was shot day wasn't it?"

"Shot day?"

"She hates them, the shots."

"What shots?" Jason said. There was a long pause. "And don't give me any crap about confidentiality." He added.

There was a dry chuckle. "Freaking ass confidentiality!" Bobby said, "You just want to know if some kid down the hall made it through surgery and they won't tell you squat." He sighed heavily, "Look there's things about Nikki you don't know."

"Like what?"

"I can't say," Bobby said, "no serious. It's like private. If she wants, she'll tell you."

"I won't tell. Heck, who would I tell anyway?"

"I know, it's not that. It's just, well it's her business. I can't tell. I promised her."

Jason lay back. He was frustrated but he could understand a personal promise. "Does she do this every time?" He asked quietly.

"Yeah, I mean Nikki cries a lot at night, but shot day, almost always. It's sad really."

CHAPTER FOUR

Hometown Hero

THE next day Alex was back and he brought pain pills at breakfast time. Shortly after breakfast he brought two assistants and bundles of gauze. They lifted his leg, unwrapped the bandages and did what they had to do. Jason kept his gaze on the far wall and talked to Alex about weight lifting. When they were done he took a nap, the pain pills plus the movement was enough to wipe him out.

When he woke Nikki was in the room again. She sat in her wheelchair, back towards the wall. She seemed happy, like her usual self. Bobby was getting up and transferring his

IV to the back of another wheelchair. As soon as he was seated he started rolling towards the door.

Jason greeted Nikki and she rolled her chair over close to his bed. "As soon as they let you up." She said conspiratorially, "I have three words for you, Off Unit Privileges."

"Off unit privileges?" He echoed.

"Ask one of the good doctors." She said.

"Good doctors?"

"Ask your rehab doctor." Bobby said from the doorway. "Your surgeon will be concerned about your picking up an infection or something, your rehab doctor will be more worried about you sitting in here all day not getting enough exercise or fresh air."

"Trust us on this," Nikki said and she rolled towards the door as well, "off unit privileges." With that they were gone.

The next time Alex came by to check on him Jason asked what off unit privileges were. Alex gave a glance towards the empty bed and rolled his eyes. "I can guess who put you up to that," he said. "We'll talk about when you can get up."

#

Jason's dad arrived later with The Village Soup, Mount Pleasant's newspaper. It wasn't much as newspaper's go, but then again it probably had a distribution that ran in the mere hundreds.

The entire town of Mt. Pleasant ran just over eight thousand and for the only newspaper that catered to local news, slow news days were the norm rather than the exception. Even on an eventful week the paper might run a couple of pages of news and the rest would be dedicated to ads for local business and various fliers.

High school sports figured large in the paper's repertoire and Jason had made the front page four times in the last year. Twice during football season his picture had been used to illustrate some game or another. The third time there had been an article about him being named most valuable player. The fourth time was this spring when a rumor had circulated that a Big Ten talent scout might be coming to watch him play in the upcoming fall season.

His father held the paper up in front of Jason and he saw he was again on the front page. His yearbook picture was on the left and next to it was a picture of him running across the field. Across the top in bold face were the words, "Hometown Hero".

Jason looked at the headline and swallowed hard. He looked at the picture of himself in his football uniform running and wondered if he would ever run again.

"Rory Underwood called the other day, concerned about you," his dad said proudly. "Then today; this!" Rory was the Village Soup's chief editor. "The article is really good." His dad went on, "and look, they are even taking up a collection to help with medical bills and rehab and stuff."

Jason started at the word "rehab" and then he thought, physical-therapy rehab, not you-got-behind-the-wheel-drunk rehab.

His father sat down and started reading the article. Jason closed his eyes and willed the pain to stop. It was worse than the dressing change by far and made even worse by the fact that his dad thought he was doing Jason a favor, helping to cheer him up.

"Jason was named Most Valuable Player last fall after the best football season since..." His father read. Would he ever run again, Jason wondered? "There was even talk of Big Ten scouts being interested..." Save your gas, Jason thought, nothing to see now.

After a couple of paragraphs about his football career the article went on to describe his "tragic accident." *Tragic?* Jason bit his lower lip. When he thought of the accident Jason used words like stupid, idiotic, and mistake.

Mom and Aunt Mandy arrived while Dad was reading. Jason had to endure another reading of the article and more fussing.

Bobby and Nikki returned just before dinner. At first Nikki looked hesitantly into the room as Bobby wheeled himself towards his bed. Jason called out to her to come in. He was glad of the diversion from the article.

The two were vague about where they had been. "Just hanging out," Nikki said. They all talked about nothing until the aide came in with Bobby's dinner. Nikki had to return to her own room to wait for her dinner and mom, dad and Aunt Mandy decided it was a good time to leave and get some dinner of their own.

The aide came back with Jason's dinner while they were saying their goodbyes. They were taking extra long to say goodbye because it was Sunday. They both had to return to work on Monday. With the hour long drive they would not be able to visit as frequently. After the article Jason was almost glad they wouldn't be here everyday. As he left Jason's dad taped the front page to the wall where everyone could see.

#

Jason felt relieved the next morning when he thought about the fact that mom and dad wouldn't be there. He would likely not have a single visitor. Family and friends meant well, but all they did was remind him just how badly he had F-ed up his life. He still didn't know if anyone knew he was drunk. He was afraid to find out. He also had no clue if he would ever walk again and he was even more afraid to ask about that. It was best to lay in bed and not think.

The feeling barely lasted through his morning dressing change. Suddenly confronted by the possibility of having nothing to do between now and the evening dressing change he felt a horrible restlessness settle on him. He couldn't move. He wasn't much of a reader and daytime television on the basic hospital cable was not a particularly enticing prospect either.

Nikki's arrival sometime mid morning was greeted enthusiastically by both boys, for a relief from boredom if nothing else. She had a short stack of DVD's in her lap.

"Okay, so this is what I got," she said holding the cases up so both could see. It was an eclectic collection of older movies. Two were collections, horror classics of the fifties and Kung fu movies from the seventies.

"Wow," Jason said sarcastically, "quite a collection."

"Hey, it's all donation out there," Nikki groused, gesturing towards the hallway, "and tons of freaking kid stuff."

Bobby nodded in agreement. "Yeah the entire collection has been donated by parents of former patients. This is about as good as it gets. Let's do horror classics." To Jason he added, "they're so corny they're actually kind of funny."

"No kung fu this time?" Nikki asked playfully.

"You nearly knocked my IV over last time." Bobby laughed, "I don't want to take no chances." He stood and took the case from Nikki.

"Fine!" She muttered and began to back her chair in between the beds so she too could see the TV screen.

"This time?" Jason asked her, "is this a special occasion or something?"

"Chemo day," she answered.

Jason looked at Bobby who shrugged, "yep, every Monday."

"Doesn't chemo make you sick and stuff?" Jason asked.

"Oh no," he replied casually, "You're thinking of the day after."

"The day after?" Jason asked.

Bobby returned from loading the DVD and sat on the side of his bed. "Chemo is pretty nasty stuff, it kills any fast growing cells. That includes hair follicles," he gestured at his scalp, "and the lining of the stomach, which is why I get so touchy and pukey. But that's tonight and tomorrow. The worst thing about today is being stuck in my room all day while they run the infusion."

"Bad movies helps the time pass," Nikki said to Jason and then to Bobby, "and it's a really good nurse day, by the way."

It was too, Jason decided as the day progressed. Angie was both Nikki's and Bobby's nurse for the day. She came in dressed in a gown with gloves and even a mask when she hung the chemo. She made Nikki scoot over to Jason's side of the room while she hung the infusion. "It's considered a biohazard." She explained.

Angie, however, did not care that Nikki kept Bobby company during the infusion. She even went as far as to bring Nikki's lunch tray into her.

Alex was Jason's nurse, and like Angie, seemed to encourage the kids to stick together. Around mid afternoon, shortly before he went off shift, he came by with a couple of bags of microwave popcorn for them. He even sat and watched part of one movie.

The movies were horrible. They were all in black and white, the special effects were ludicrous, and none were scary. However, listening to Nikki and Bobby bad mouth the movies was priceless.

"Now why is she going back in there?" Nikki complained, "you know two girls have already been killed! Just run, stupid!"

"She's getting a little worked up, Bobby," Jason joked.

"Yeah," Bobby agreed, "she does that. Why do you think I vetoed the Kung Fu movies?"

Nikki made an exasperated noise, "well, wouldn't you run?"

"Yes," Bobby agreed, "I would, it's okay."

"Well, I wouldn't. Or perhaps I should say, couldn't" Jason said with a look at his leg.

Nikki blushed suddenly, "I am sorry, I didn't mean..."

"It's a joke," He said interrupting her. He started laughing suddenly. He couldn't explain to anyone, even himself, why it struck him as so funny but it did. He had the image of dragging himself along the ground, trying to escape a serial killer. He laughed so hard and so long that Nikki eventually banged her wheelchair loudly into his bed and called him a dork, which only made him laugh harder.

It was late afternoon before the evening shift nurse stuck her head in and told Nikki she needed to return to her own room. The third movie of the day was winding down anyway.

"So Nikki," Jason began in what he hoped was a casual voice, "Bobby over there has cancer. I have a messed up leg. What's your story? You dying of cancer?" He said it jokingly but he saw her stiffen.

"Nope," she replied through tight lips, "not dying."

"I was just kidding," he said, suddenly sorry.

"I know." She said rolling towards the door.

Jason looked over at Bobby helplessly. Bobby gave him a doleful look. "Bye Nikki," Bobby called after her, "see you tomorrow maybe?"

"Yeah, maybe," She replied.

"Bye," Jason put in as well. She did not respond.

When she was gone Bobby said, "why did you go and do that, bro?"

Jason looked at him and said, "I'm sorry. I was just asking a question."

"Didn't I tell you it's private." Bobby replied angrily. "If she wants you to know, she'll tell you. Don't go prying."

"But I don't understand," Jason complained.

"Do you have to?" Bobby responded.

"No," Jason retorted, "but, you're dying."

"And your point is?" Bobby said.

"You're dying. I'll probably never walk again." It spilled out of him before he could stop it.

There was a long pause. He looked over and found Bobby staring at his leg. "Is it that bad, bro?" Bobby whispered.

Jason shook his head yes. Then not wanting to talk about it further he said, "my point is she can talk about you dying, or my leg, like it's no big deal. What's so terrible about her that she can't say it?"

Bobby looked at him hard. He said slowly, "It's not a good or bad sort of thing with Nikki, it's just really private. And she don't want to talk." He lay back in the bed and fluffed his pillow. "If she don't come around tomorrow because of you, I am going to be pissed, bro."

CHAPTER FIVE

The Day After Chemo Day

JASON woke to the sound of Bobby vomiting noisily in the shared bathroom. His first thought was, day after chemo day. His second thought was, I wonder if Nikki will come by today? It made him sad. He hadn't meant anything by the question.

Okay, so he did mean something. Why didn't Nikki want to talk about why she was here? Why wouldn't anyone else say anything? The nurses he could sort of understand. It was part of their code or something. But Bobby knew something. Why wouldn't Bobby talk? What could be so terrible?

The sound of retching went on. "You okay

in there?" Jason called after awhile, "You want me to call a nurse or something?"

"There's a call light in here," Bobby answered. He still sounded irritated.

Jason blushed, chagrined. How was he supposed to know that? He hadn't left his bed, except on a cart, since arriving. Was he supposed to be the hospital expert suddenly?

Bobby started coming out of the bathroom about the same time a nurse aide came in with breakfast. Bobby took the barest glance at the tray and disappeared back into the bathroom.

"Is he going to be okay?" He asked Melinda, the nurse's aide that brought his tray.

"Yeah, don't worry." She assured him, "chemo makes his stomach really sensitive. Even the smell of food is enough to set it off."

It was hard to enjoy breakfast to the sound of dry heaves, Jason thought sourly as he bit into the egg biscuit he had been brought. But it was harder still knowing that the smell of your breakfast was what was making the kid sick to begin with. Still, what could he do? He was starving and not about to go without for Bobby's sake.

He thought briefly about whether or not it would be better if he requested a different room, so Bobby wouldn't have to smell his food every day after chemo. There were two problems. Bobby might misinterpret it, he might think that Jason didn't want to be his roommate anymore. Jason didn't want him to think that.

Besides they might put Jason into a private room. They were suppose to put him in a private room, if they hadn't been full when he arrived. Now that he had met Bobby and Nikki, he didn't want that. He feared they wouldn't come visit him. He would be forced to lay by himself in bed day after day.

Jason finished his meal quickly and then called the nurse to come take it away immediately. Melinda gave him an understanding look when she came for the tray. Bobby had passed by the bed holding his nose and trying to apologize for holding his nose. Jason told him not to worry about it.

Alex came by a little time later and did Jason's dressing change. Jason kept his eyes forward, still not looking at what was left of his leg. The only problem with this was that his eyes kept falling on the paper his dad had hung up on the cork board by his bedside. He glared at the headline but it refused to go away.

Afterwards he tried to get comfortable, to take a nap like he had been doing after the morning routine. He couldn't. He felt irritable and out of sorts. He was restless.

Bobby got up and made yet another dash for the bathroom. After several minutes worth of dry heaves he reappeared in the doorway. He looked pale and gaunt.

"Hey," Jason said, "can I ask a small favor?"

Bobby shrugged.

"Can you grab that paper there?" Jason said pointing at his hometown hero headline.

Bobby shuffled over, dragging his IV pole behind him. "Want to read your article?" Jason detected a sarcastic undertone in the comment as Bobby handed him the paper.

While Bobby made his way around Jason's bed and towards his own, Jason quickly folded the paper into fourths. He stretched his arms to reach the bedside table. It was awkward, the table was at his head level and he couldn't shift his leg, so he ended up reaching around and almost upside down to open the top drawer. He shoved the paper in and slammed the door shut.

"Guess you didn't want to read the article," Bobby commented as he sat down on his bed. Jason noticed the tone was softer. "Do you want to talk about it?" Bobby asked.

Jason shook his head, "not really. You feeling better?"

"Less nauseous," Bobby replied, "but wiped, man."

"They still giving you stuff? I mean I see you've still got the IV thing running." Jason said.

"Just fluids," Bobby replied looking up at the bag. "I can't even keep water down most of the time after chemo and they don't want me to dehydrate. Besides it helps with the nausea a little bit and they can give me IV meds for the nausea too if I need them."

Bobby lay back down. "I got written up in the local paper too, you know." He said quietly from his bed.

Jason stared at the ceiling for a long time before answering. "Did they call you a hero?"

"Yup," was the reply.

After another long pause Jason asked, "did you feel like a hero?"

Bobby considered this for a long time. "No," he said finally. "I felt like I was dying of cancer." Jason felt a weight lift from his heart.

#

Not long after lunchtime Alex appeared in Jason's room with a wheelchair. One of it's footrests had been set perpendicular. A couple of aides were following in Alex's wake.

"What's that contraption?" Jason asked nodding towards the chair.

"You're wheelchair." Alex said.

"Mine?"

"Yes," Alex replied firmly, "It's time to get you up."

"Up!" Jason said feeling frightened. "I'm suppose to walk or something?"

"No," Alex said, "but you do need to get up. The worst thing for the body is being immobile. Every day you lay in bed you are losing muscle mass, bone density and running a risk for infections, blood clots, you name it."

From laying in bed? Alex looked serious.

"I am serious," Alex said. "They spend like a whole week in your first semester of nursing school just underscoring that one point. Laying in bed doing nothing is the worse thing a patient can do. It leads to complications. You need to rest your leg so it can heal, but you also need to keep the rest of your body working, so when that leg heals your body will still be strong."

"Okay coach," Jason joked.

Alex smiled. "That's the spirit. Here's what we are going to do. We are going to get you up and into this wheelchair. Then I am taking you down to physical therapy. They'll start working with you on some exercises for the rest of your body."

Getting into the wheelchair seemed adventure enough for Jason, who couldn't move his leg. Alex removed one of the side rests from the chair so they could slide it right next to the bed. They made Jason sit up in his bed. He winced slightly as the aides lifted his leg. While the two aides held his leg steady a couple of inches off the bed, Jason scooted slowly towards the edge. Alex helped guide Jason's hand and braced the chair while Jason hoisted his butt across and into the seat.

Jason had a fine sheen of sweat on his face by the time he was in the chair. Less than a week ago he had been running wind sprints across the high school football field, now sitting in a chair took every ounce of energy he had.

"It's not going to hurt anything...there," he gestured nervously at the bandages around his thigh.

"Don't worry, you'll be fine." Alex said.

Jason looked around. Bobby was snoring on his side of the room. Jason wanted to tell him, "hey, look I am up," or something but he didn't want to wake him either. Bobby had looked so wiped out earlier.

The room looked and felt different from this vantage point. His leg hurt and despite Alex's reassurances each twinge scared him. How could he be sure he wasn't tearing something? Still it was good to know that there were other parts of his body that worked. It gave him a tiny bit of hope. The thought of physical therapy too gave him hope, hope that he could redeem himself. He would work hard and maybe he would be the hometown hero after all.

The hall was a new experience for Jason. He had heard the bustle at times and the stillness at other times. But he had virtually no visual to go with the sounds until now.

To his left the hallway led deeper into the unit. Somewhere down that way, he had been told, was a patient lounge area with play areas for the younger patients. (He knew this because the younger kids often annoyed Bobby but Nikki enjoyed playing with them and helping them.)

Directly in front of him as he was wheeled out of his room was another door, Nikki's room. That door was currently closed. He was disappointed. His last chance to share his new-found mobility was gone. Was she napping too?

To his right he saw a man approaching. The man wore street clothes, dress slacks and a button down shirt over a bulging gut. He had a slouched posture, as though a weight rested on him. It was not the dress or the posture that drew Jason's attention, but the face. It was narrow and pinched. The hair was nut brown and short. The resemblance was unmistakable.

Sure enough the man turned at Nikki's door just as Jason was wheeled past and away. With a sense of deja vue Jason craned his head to catch the interaction as he rolled down the hallway and away.

"Hey, Nick, you there?" The man said at the door. Nikki's voice answered but Jason could not make out what she said.

Nick? It seemed odd that her dad would shorten her name like that.

Physical therapy quickly drove any thought of Nikki from his mind. It was as if the accident had sapped all of his energy. He was strong, even off season he worked out regularly and kept in good shape. But doing even the most basic things with a leg that was weighted down with metal spikes and stuck out in front of him was awkward.

He got through it. The physical therapist had him slide out of the chair and onto an exam table of sorts. He lay there and the therapist put his left leg, now his good leg, through a series of exercises. Then they practiced some common things, like getting into and out of the wheelchair. He made Jason roll the wheelchair himself, driving through an obstacle course around the therapy department.

Nikki's door was closed when he rolled past on his way back to his room. As they turned the corner he spied her in their room talking to Bobby. He smiled, glad that she had not avoided Bobby because of Jason's stupidity.

"You're up," Nikki said as he rolled in, "That's great."

"I am not so sure," he groused slightly, but he felt happy, "That physical therapist put me through the wringer."

"It will get easier every time." Alex said from behind him. "You gonna sit up a while or get back in bed?"

He wanted to sit up, if only to show Nikki and Bobby he could, but his leg ached fiercely. "I think I'd better get back in bed for awhile," he replied timidly with an almost sheepish glance at Bobby and Nikki.

"Yeah," Nikki said, coming to his rescue, "don't push it the first day."

Alex and an aide helped support Jason's bad leg while he transferred himself over to the bed. He let out an involuntary groan as he settled into the bed. He looked over at Nikki, embarrassed.

When the nurse was gone with Jason's wheelchair Nikki rolled over to his bed. She produced a pudding cup from within her lap somewhere.

"Vanilla," she said. "Its the only choice you get on day after chemo day. It's the only thing that doesn't make him puke."

"That's fine," Jason said with a smile, "I like vanilla too."

As Nikki backed her chair against the wall he remembered the scene from earlier, Nikki's dad at the door saying "Nick, you there?" He glanced over at Bobby and felt a sudden sense of normalcy. The three of them in the room, eating pudding. It was his anchor. He wasn't about to ruin it with mysteries.

CHAPTER SIX

The Rules for Being Nikki

JASON'S life was quickly falling into a pattern. The hospital ran on patterns, three shifts changing like clockwork, rotating staff schedules and doctor's rounds. At first each seemed random but if you stuck around the patterns emerged, who had what days off, which doctors came early, which doctors came late.

In Jason's own case the major patterns were obvious and apparent. The dressing change on what was left of his thigh marked the beginning and end of each day. Meal came at regular times. In between was physical therapy and afternoon visits with Nikki and

Bobby. When Nikki and Bobby were not around there were long stretches of staring at white walls or watching TV shows that no longer seemed to have any connection to any life that Jason might contemplate.

His parents came when they could but it was an hour drive and they had other responsibilities. Besides it was not like he was dying. He knew he shouldn't be resentful but it was hard not to be. They weren't the ones stuck in a hospital.

Aunt Mandy was his most regular visitor. She came three or four times a week. She brought stacks of books for Nikki and Nikki devoured them almost as fast. On Nikki's suggestion Jason had started on a popular fantasy series, but he wasn't nearly as much of a reader as she was. Aunt Mandy would also pick up movies sometimes or games that he and Bobby could play together on Bobby's Xbox.

His mom had brought the iPad Jason had gotten for Christmas with her on one of her first trips up. He had been excited to see it at first. Now it mostly stayed in the bedside drawer only to be brought out when he was in a dark morbid mood.

Today was such a day. Bobby was gone having tests. Today had been another shot day for Nikki, so he didn't expect to see her at all. He had pulled out his iPad and was flipping through his Facebook page.

Time was passing outside the hospital as

though nothing life-changing had occurred. It was three weeks into summer vacation and his classmates were going on vacations, enjoying the beach and having cookouts.

His friends left messages from time to time, or chatted if they were online. The messages were encouraging, hopeful things. Get better soon.

He mostly ignored the messages. They were meaningless to him. What was important were the pictures. Pictures of his friend Ron in shorts, with lean healthy looking legs. Pictures of Dan swinging from a rope over the swimming hole where they had hung out since middle school. Jenny in a bikini at the pool. James in Iowa City running a 5k. Hundreds of pictures of hundreds of teens all doing perfectly normal teen stuff. Stuff Jason would probably never do again.

The worst part was that they were all still drinking. He knew. There were enough parents on Facebook and his friends were smart enough not to say so, or to post pictures with beer in sight. They didn't have to. He saw bonfires at night, slack faces, broad smiles and glassy eyes. That was enough. They were still drinking and partying as though his accident had never happened. Or more likely, as though what happened to him would never happen to them.

Jason had no illusions about himself. He hadn't listen to any of the countless public service messages on TV or at school about the dangers of driving drunk. Why should he? That sort of stuff happened to other people in faraway places.

And now Jason had found yet another torment for himself. Jeydon Holmes, a t-shirt hanging loosely over his slender chest, sitting on a picnic table out at Oakland Mills Park. Next to him, in a bikini, was Jason's girlfriend Brittany.

It was a group outing, he told himself. It could be no more than an innocent coincidence that they were side by side in this picture. Side by side, not together. It probably meant nothing.

But then why hadn't Brittany posted any pictures from this particular outing? She had posted plenty of other pictures. Why hadn't she mentioned the outing in any of her phone calls?

What did he expect anyway? Jason wasn't stupid. He knew the score. In middle school he'd been this dorky boy who liked video games, a nobody. No girl wanted anything to do with him.

His freshman year of high school his coach "saw promise" in the wiry little kid. During his sophomore year he had a growth spurt and started putting on some real muscle. He started plowing through the line again and again. He led the JV squad to victory more than once and towards the end of the season he was being put in the varsity games.

And everything changed. Suddenly all the

other boys were clapping him on the shoulder in hall and calling out his name to sit with them at lunch. Anything he did was 'cool'. Adult men would shake his hand on the street and comment about the games.

That was nothing compared to the girls. It was like someone had flipped a switch and every girl in school had noticed him at once. They blushed when he looked at them in class. They whispered about him in the hallways. At parties they came up to him, vying for his attention. He was a catch, the star football player. Now he was on his way to being a nobody again.

He sighed. He couldn't even get mad at Brittany. This was not what she had signed on for. She had wanted to be with the most popular kid in school. Jason was that kid. Now he wasn't and she would move on.

Her choice made that clear. Jeydon was a little taller than Jason and a lot thinner. He played on the team as wide receiver. Without Jason, he was their best hope for the next year.

There was a sound at the door and Jason looked up. An aide was wheeling Bobby through the door in a wheelchair. Jason sat the iPad aside, glad for a distraction from his morbid thoughts.

The next day when Jason got back from his morning rehab session he felt good enough that he told Alex he would stay up in his wheelchair until after lunch. It was the first time and Alex seemed pleased with the news.

Bobby was gone again. Jason wheeled over to his side of the room and manage to fish one of the Xbox controllers out from under the TV set and rolled back into position. He booted up the most recent Gods of War game and set it to single player.

There was a knock at the door and Jason looked up. A man stood in the doorway. He was tall and slender. He wore dress slacks and a blue button down shirt. Over this was a white lab jacket, the pockets loaded down with pens, a pocket book and a wide assortment of medical instruments that Jason could not identify.

"Hey, I'm Dr. Jan," the man said from the doorway, "mind if I come in Jason?"

Jason paused the game and nodded. Another doctor? He thought. Out loud he said, "So what do you do?"

"You don't remember?" Dr. Jan said as he sat on the edge of Jason's bed. "We've met," he explained, "but that was just after your accident and you were still pretty out of it. Since then I have been involved in your case but I haven't really needed to see you. I am head of the rehab department. Alex and Greg report to me regularly about your progress."

Rehab? That sparked something at the back of Jason's mind. He tried to think what.

"Anyway," the doctor continued, "It looks like things are going fairly well but I thought it was time to stop by and see what you thought."

Unsure how he was supposed to answer, Jason looked around the room. He saw Bobby's empty unmade bed and a conversation came back to him.

"Umm, rehab?" Jason said. "I was sort of thinking, Greg," Greg was his physical therapist, "is always urging me to the do the exercises and stuff whenever I think about them, three, four times a day even. And to push myself in the wheelchair too."

"Yes," Dr. Jan agreed, "One therapy session is nothing compared to laying in bed all day. I am encouraged to see you up. You really need to work at being active."

"Yeah, so I was thinking if I could have off unit privileges that might help." Jason said.

Dr. Jan raised an eyebrow. Jason plunged on, "I mean if I could get out in the hallway and wheel myself around that would be great exercise. And I can get in and out of bed myself these days. I would be doing that more often if there was somewhere I could go. Even down to the patient lounge would be nice, but around the hospital would be even better."

Dr. Jan shrugged, "I'll talk to your nurse about it but I don't see a problem. It's good to work with motivated patients. I'm not surprised. I find ball players among the most motivated of the patients I see."

Jason's heart sank. He nodded.

"I hear you had quite the high school career. Some talk of college ball even." Dr. Jan said.

Jason nodded again.

"I see quite a few of the University team," Dr. Jan went on, "I could maybe arrange for some of them to come visit if you would like?'

Jason nodded again, "Sure." He paused a long time and said, "do you think?" He stopped. "Do you think I'll ever?" He broke off again.

Dr. Jan reached over and put one hand on Jason's arm. "I am going to help you regain as much mobility and use as I can. Know that. Right now neither the ortho doc nor the vascular surgeon want us to do anything with that leg." he pointed at Jason's right leg as he spoke. "Later we'll start exercising it and we'll see. I wish I could tell you more, but that's where we stand right now."

Jason nodded dully.

"You just keep working hard in therapy okay?" Dr. Jan said rising, "And I'll talk to the nurse about off unit privileges, deal?"

"Deal." Jason answered.

Just a few minutes later Alex came in, a grin on his face. "So somebody got their off unit privileges." He said.

I did not get an answer about my leg, Jason thought. He shoved the thought down. "Yeah," he said.

Alex sat on Jason's bed. "Now the first thing you need to know is this; off unit privileges are a privilege. You abuse them, they will be taken away. You follow the rules, you keep them, understand?

Jason nodded. Alex quickly recited off the rules. He was to always check in with his nurse before leaving the unit, to make sure he wasn't missing any tests or appointments. He was to be back at meal times and change of shift. He was confined to the hospital grounds and to the public places within the hospital. He was not to be on any other unit or in any treatment areas. He was not to be disruptive or block traffic.

When he was done Alex said, "any questions?"

"Umm," Jason glanced at Bobby's empty bed.

Alex chuckled. "Nikki asked me to break a five," Alex said, "So I am guessing you will find the two of them in the main lobby by the vending machines."

"Thanks." Jason said.

Navigating the hallway by himself in the wheelchair proved harder than Jason would have imagined. Still he managed to make it to the bank of elevators and down to main level. From there it was a short roll into the wide main lobby.

The vending machines were set in a semi-separate dining area just off the main lobby. As Jason started rolling towards it he heard his name being called.

"Jason! Over here!" It was Nikki. She and Bobby were on the opposite side of the lobby. She was in her wheelchair as usual and Bobby was sitting on one of the couches. He waved back and made towards them.

"Got your walking papers I see," Nikki said with a grin as he pulled up.

"Yup," he replied, "the rehab guy stopped by and I remembered what you guys said about off unit privileges. He agreed."

"Awesome," Bobby said. He did not however seem quite as enthused as Nikki was.

A man walked by. He was dressed in slacks and a dress shirt. Jason looked down at himself. He had an extra baggy pair of scrub pants on (they had to be extra baggy to get over the metal pins in his leg) with one leg cut off to make room for his dressing. He had a faded old gray T shirt on. Nikki was dressed in navy blue scrubs, like always. Bobby had on sweatpants and a T shirt, plus a bathrobe against the cold. (Not that it was cold to anyone but Bobby.) He also wore his signature blue stocking cap.

It was normal attire for them. For the last three weeks it was just how Jason saw the three of them. Now, sitting in the lobby surrounded by "normal" people in street clothes he was suddenly embarrassed by how they must look.

"So what you guys up to?" Jason asked.

Nikki held up a 20 oz. Coke.

"Looks good," Jason said.

"Want to get something?" Bobby asked. He had a sprite next him.

Jason looked down at his scrubs. "Umm,

well I don't have money with me."

"It's okay," Nikki said, "I got a couple extra to keep in my room for later." She pulled a second coke out that she had tucked in beside in her wheelchair. She held it out to him.

"I can hit you back later," Jason said taking the coke.

"Don't worry," Nikki said, "just consider it payback for the books and stuff. I really appreciate it."

"They're library books." Jason said. "I'll pay you back."

"It's not necessary" Nikki insisted. Jason let it drop but promised himself he would pay her back.

"So what's the big attraction?" He said looking around the lobby.

"It's not the unit," Bobby replied sardonically.

"Well," Nikki said, "so far today we've been to our favorite restaurant, Vendy's, and then we did some window shopping at the mall." She pointed to the tiny gift shop in one corner of the lobby, "and now we are people watching in the plaza." She spread her arms wide.

Jason chuckled. He looked around. "So anything good in the mall?"

They both shrugged. "Not really." Bobby answered. "And it's way too expensive."

"You can always dream, right?" Nikki said. "We can go back if you want. You up to it,

Bobby?"

Bobby shrugged.

"Don't bother on my account," Jason said. "With this monstrosity," he gestured at his right leg, perpendicular in front of him, "I won't be able to navigate that tiny space anyway."

He backed in next to Nikki so he could face the gift shop at least. "We can just look through the windows." I might as well get used to living my life that way, he thought to himself.

He followed Nikki's gaze. "That would look nice on you." He commented.

She gave him a clouded look. A look that if he were forced to interpret it he would say was about how he had felt looking at Facebook earlier.

"What would look nice?" Bobby asked craning his head.

"The pink top." He said, mystified.

"That would be against the rules." Nikki said in a small voice.

"What? We aren't allowed to buy things from the gift shop?" Jason asked. Bobby shot him a warning glance.

"No," Nikki replied quietly, "It would be against the rules for being Nikki."

"Rules for being Nikki?" It was out of his mouth before he could stop himself.

"There aren't rules for being Jason?" She asked sarcastically.

"Umm," he felt completely out of his depth.

"Rules about what you can and can not wear?" She went on, not looking at him, "Rules about what kind of activities are appropriate? What colors your room can be? What toys you can or can not have?"

She didn't seem to be talking to him directly, which was good because he had no idea how to answer any of it.

His mom got after him if he didn't dress up for a family gathering or his dad got mad if he was out past curfew but he didn't think these were the sort of rules that Nikki was talking about.

"I'm sorry," she said looking back at him. "It's just always been like that. There has always been a ton of rules I have to follow, as long as I can remember."

"What are your parents control freaks or something?" Jason asked. He thought momentarily maybe that was it. Maybe they were mental case control freaks and abusive. Maybe they had hurt Nikki somehow and that's why she was here but didn't want to talk about it. Maybe they were waiting on placement in a foster home. Then he remember the man, her father, that had visited the other day. If he was abusive they wouldn't have let him visit, would they?

"It's not like that." Nikki said shaking her head, "it's just always been this way. They aren't trying to be mean or anything. It's me. The rules for being Nikki, they're rules you've probably always followed without anyone telling you or nothing. I've got some sort of brain glitch where I can't see what's obvious to everyone else."

He looked at her, trying to process her answer. She looked up and said. "Guys, it's almost lunchtime we'd better be getting back."

Jason followed the two of them out of the lobby. Bobby, who no longer had his IV pole, walked at the front. Behind him came Nikki in her wheelchair with Jason at the tail end. Bobby led them down a different hallway then the one Jason had come in from. When they reached the bank of service elevators Jason grasped his logic. Both wheelchairs would not fit into a regular sized elevator together.

As they neared the ward the hallway was wide enough and traffic light enough that Jason pulled up alongside Nikki.

"We'll show you one of our other places tomorrow." Nikki said. "Maybe the the outpatient lobby. They have this huge glass wall. There is a second floor balcony area too. You can sit up there and look outside and it's almost like you've been out of the hospital."

Bobby snorted, "sure almost."

Jason grinned, "I'll take almost right now." He said. Then he stopped, noticing the look on Nikki's face.

Her face was tight. Her eyes had narrowed suspiciously. Her lips were a tight frown. Jason followed her gaze onto the unit.

There was an older man standing in the hall in front of Nikki's room. He was tall, thin and angular. He had gray hair that was thinning on top. He was wearing a brown tweed suit.

Beside every door there was a small supply closet that Jason had heard the nurses refer to as "nurse servers". They contained medical supplies, some linens, a fold down tray and the medical chart. Nurses and doctors alike would fold down the tray and open the chart to read or write notes. Which was exactly what this man had been doing. He had Nikki's chart out on the tray. He picked it up as they all approached him.

"Well, well," he said with an insincere smile. "If it isn't my favorite patient, Nic-"

"Nikki," Nikki said in tone somewhere between demanding and pleading.

"Of course," he said, "You wish to go by Nikki now." He gestured towards her room. "May we talk?"

Nikki looked over at Jason and gave him a quiet "see you." She made a similar sound towards Bobby.

All this time Bobby was staring at Jason. He had a sharp irritated look on his face, a look that Jason read to mean, "Now is not the time to open your big fat mouth and ask a stupid question." Jason kept his mouth shut.

After watching Nikki disappear into her room, followed by the man, Jason rolled into his own room. Bobby followed.

Bobby sat upright on the edge of his bed while Jason transferred himself back into his own bed. When Jason was back in bed Bobby came over and sat in Jason's wheelchair.

In a low voice he said, "remember how we've told you there are good doctors and bad doctors?"

Jason nodded.

"That is a bad doctor." Bobby said gravely.

"You warned me," Jason said, "and I've seen it for myself. That surgeon that did my leg? Everyone swears he's the best. But when he comes, he's a plain ass. If you ask a question he looks at you like you are stupid or something. I think he means well but he has no clue how to deal with a patient that's awake."

"True," Bobby said. "But that doctor," he pointed across the hall, "is Nikki's psychiatrist and I do not believe he means well."

With that he got up and returned to his bed. Lunch arrived only moments later and the two ate in silence. They did not see Nikki again that day.

CHAPTER SEVEN

Nicholas

THE next morning when Alex came to get him for therapy, Jason waved him off. "Let me do it," he said.

Alex smiled and parked the wheelchair against the side of Jason's bed and stepped back. He looked on encouragingly as Jason scooted himself over and used his arms to lift and pull his butt onto the chair. Then he reached down and grabbed just below his knee. Bracing himself for the inevitable stab of pain, he hoisted his leg over and onto the waiting footrest, already set out perpendicular. He let out a sigh as the leg settled into place.

"Awesome," Alex said from where he

stood by the wall. He took a step forward but Jason held up his hand.

"I've got to learn, I guess." Jason said as he released the brakes and started himself forward.

"That attitude will get you far," Alex said clapping him on the back as Jason rolled towards the hallway.

Another nurse, Andrea, was going into Nikki's room as Jason pulled out into the hallway. The door was halfway open and he could hear them talking inside. What was more, she had left the nurse server open and Nikki's chart was propped in it's cubbyhole. He caught one glimpse and his heart stopped.

"Pagan, Nicholas" It said along the back spine.

He kept rolling, not daring to stop and confirm what he had seen. How could he? All the nurses had made it clear that they could not share any information about other patients, even Alex had been firm on that point. Nikki had made it abundantly clear that she did not want anyone knowing more about her case than absolutely necessary.

Jason was glad when they reached the elevator doors and he could pause and think.

"Is something wrong?" Alex asked at his side.

"No," Jason lied, "Just kind of spacey."

He stared at the steel doors. Nikki's real name was not Nicole, it was Nicholas. There was her dad, turning in the door and saying

"Hey Nick." He had not misheard. Did that mean Nikki was a boy?

He started to get angry. She had lied to him. No, *he* had lied to Jason. Maybe. Had Nikki ever actually said she was a girl? He tried to think back but he could not think of a single time when she said, "I am a girl." She had said and done plenty that had led him to think she was a girl. The name Nikki was feminine. She acted feminine. But had she ever said it? He wasn't sure.

Bobby referred to Nikki as *she* and he seemed to know something about her, him. Did he know that Nikki's real name was Nicholas? What was going on? Was Bobby lying to him too? Or was he too being duped. The more Jason thought about the more confusing it was.

There was a bing and the doors slid open. Jason waited while the elevator unloaded and then backed himself in. All the while he kept thinking what he had seen.

He thought about the other day in the lobby, the rules for being Nikki. They made more sense now. A pink shirt was against 'the rules' because Nikki was really a boy. Was Nikki like those kids you saw on TV sometimes, trans-whatever it was - boys who want be girls? Was that why her parents had placed all those rules on her? If so what was she doing here?

Maybe she was having her operation to become a girl, he thought. He immediately dismissed the idea. She couldn't be having a sex change operation without her parent's approval, and they wouldn't have a bunch of rules against being girly if they approved of it, would they?

Besides he had no real proof that Nikki was a boy. Nor did he have any proof that if she was a boy, she was trying to be a girl. There might be another explanation entirely. He thought back to his Nikki's-been-abused theory. Maybe the parents wanted a boy so they gave their daughter a male name and forced her to act like a boy. It seemed far fetched, but no more so than any other theory at this point.

There also seemed to be a distinct possibility that there was something mentally wrong with Nikki. I mean a hospital counselor had stopped by and talked to Jason. Bobby got regular visits from the grief counselors. Nikki had a psychiatrist. That was a lot more serious, in Jason's mind. Maybe Nikki was like a pet name, or a child's name, some sort of regression Nikki was going through.

"Hey," Greg greeted him in the therapy department, "You look a million miles away."

He nodded, not sure how to answer.

"Well, you better get your head in the game," Greg said, "I've got some new exercises I want you to work on."

Jason nodded, pushing the thought of Nikki down.

#

Bobby was rolling out of their room in a wheelchair as Jason rounded the corner to the unit.

"Tests, again." Bobby said to the unspoken question.

"God, as many tests as you've taken you should have a college degree by now." Jason joked.

"I've certainly got the medical lingo down." Bobby replied sardonically. He held his hand out, mirroring Jason's hand. They gave each other a high five as they passed. Jason thought he caught a half smile on Bobby's face as he passed out of sight.

Jason spun into his room and nearly crashed into Nikki, who was heading out. He stopped momentarily.

She was the same Nikki as always, the same blue hospital scrubs, the same shaggy reddish-brown hair, the same pinched face. But his view of her had changed.

How old was she? Younger than either him or Bobby, but older than the other kids on the unit. Fourteen? Fifteen? She was flat chested. How many of the girls at his high school were still flat at that age? A few at least but not many. Her hair was shaggy. Was it a feminine cut? Or a masculine cut that had grown out? Nothing about her was certain.

Then their eyes met. He saw, in the brown depths, an incredible sadness. He thought suddenly of her crying herself to sleep at night. Any anger he had felt at being deceived, if he had in fact been deceived about something, evaporated. Any accusations he had thought of went out the window.

She looked down suddenly, as if aware that she had revealed something. He blinked.

"You don't have to run off." He said, "Back up and let me through." He tried to sound cheerful, she looked like she needed it.

Dutifully she backed up and he swung into the room. After a few minutes of maneuvering they managed to get both chairs facing the TV and backed into a position where they were side by side.

"So what's new?" He asked. It sounded incredibly stupid the second it left his mouth and he cursed at himself.

She just shrugged, "Not much, and you?"

He shrugged too. "Therapy went okay. Other than that, not much new."

They sat in an awkward silence for awhile. Not knowing quite what motivated him, Jason turned in his chair and fished the newspaper out of his bedside drawer and handed it to Nikki. "This is my hometown paper," he said.

She read in silence for awhile and then said, "Wow, this is really cool, Jason. You are like the star football player."

"Was," Jason corrected.

"You are a hero, people look up to you." Nikki insisted. "Why do you hide this in a drawer? You should put this out where people can see it."

"No." He replied.

She gave him a sharp look. "Why not?"

"I am not a hero." He said.

She scanned the page again, "just look at all the people they quote, Jason." She said. "You must have a ton of friends."

"I am not a hero." He repeated firmly. He stared at his leg, not wanting to look up at Nikki's face. "Nikki, trust me, I am not a hero. I, I was drunk."

"Drunk?" She asked.

"The night I crashed my car, I had been to a party. I had been drinking." He said, "I was way too drunk to drive. I knew it. It was stupid. I made a stupid mistake and now I've f-ed up my life forever." He turned and gave Nikki a dry sarcastic smile. "Sound like a hero to you?"

He looked away quickly, fighting against tears. He felt a small hand on his back. "Jason," Nikki said.

"No," he replied, "You don't belong here. Bobby doesn't belong here. Neither of you has done anything and yet you're both stuck here. Me, I belong. I did this to myself. I deserve it, all of it."

"Don't say that," she said sharply.

"Why not? It's true. I f-ed up."

"Bullshit!" She said. "You deserve to be grounded for two weeks or something. Not crippled for life."

After that he broke down completely. Nikki's small hand guided him towards her and she held his head while he cried. Once he saw

Alex out of the corner of his eye appear and then, catching the scene, disappear again.

A few minutes later he was able to pull himself together. "I"m sorry." He said.

She smacked him playfully upside the head, "Dork." She said. "Crying is nothing to be ashamed of, especially after what you've been through. You nearly died."

#

"Frag him! Frag him!" Jason yelled at Bobby as he propelled his fighter back, jumping the barricade behind which Bobby's fighter was hiding. As he jumped he saw a fragmentation grenade fly across the corner of the screen. He watched the kill shot on Bobby's half of the screen and then took his eyes off the screen long enough to give him a high five.

They were playing Halo on Xbox live. Andrea "McBitch", as Nikki called her, had shooed Nikki out of their room early in the afternoon. Bobby had come back from his tests around supper time. After supper Bobby had suggested starting an online game. Jason had seen some names he knew, people from back home, and they had challenged them.

"Man, you are wiping the floor with us tonight," Dan said in Jason's ear-piece. Jason and Dan had been friends for years and Jason could easily visualize Dan's heavy form sitting on the tattered couch in the basement den of his house. Jason had nearly grown up on that couch, playing Gamecube games as a child, graduating to the PS2 and then the Xbox.

"What can I say?" Jason responded lightly, maneuvering his on-screen fighter where he could see beyond the barricade but still had some cover, "I'm playing with cancer boy. Everyone knows cancer boys are the best gamers out there. They got nothing better to do."

"Dude!" Another voice interrupted, "Can you say that shit?"

Jason gave a sidelong glance at Bobby, who was laughing too hard to answer. Jason smiled. It was one of the tricks Nikki had taught him. What Bobby wanted, more than anything else, was for people to treat his condition like it was no big deal. Bobby finally stopped laughing long enough to reassure the other players that he was cool with Jason's assessment of his gaming skill.

The last kill had been particularly satisfying for Jason. "Jey-Jey-Binks" was the Xbox user id for Jeydon, the boy who was most likely stealing his girlfriend.

As if on cue Jeydon's voice came on the headset, "I gotta get off after this game anyway. You'll have to find someone else to beat."

Jason glanced at the clock. Eight PM. "Is there a party?" He asked casually.

There was a long awkward pause. "Not really," Jeydon answered, "A few of us are getting together out at Bingham's farm."

Bingham's farm. It was about ten miles down the road from where his accident had been. Jason knew Bingham's farm all too well. They held bonfires out there all the time. And Keggers.

Jason caught a glimpse of something on the screen. He reset his weapon to a rocket launcher. There was the movement again. It was Dan's fighter. Jason opened fire, blowing away most of the wall Dan was hiding behind.

"Whoa, that was overkill." Dan said.

"Wouldn't want you late for the party," Jason joked savagely.

"Whateve-" Jeydon said and "Jey-Jey-Binks" went offline.

"I'm not going anyway," Dan said sullenly.

"Why not?" Jason replied, hoping he sounded casual. "It'll probably be the biggest party of the summer, if I know Josh." He was referring to Joshua Bingham. "It'll be fun."

"Yeah," Dan said and Jason caught a hint of real emotion behind the words, "but it won't be the same with my best friend in hospital."

Jason sighed, "I know what you mean."

Jason had been a nobody in elementary and middle school. It hadn't been until high school and football that anyone noticed him. Dan on the other hand had been worse than a nobody. He had been overweight since kindergarten and had always been picked on. He was also (how to say it politely?) not the brightest.

In high school he put on enough muscle to put his weight to work on the offensive line. Being on the football team had put Dan on the map but it was only his friendship with Jason that put him in the A crowd.

Dan suggested they team up and find someone else to play against but Jason said, "Naw, it's not that long before they'll come around to do my leg again and then it's "quiet time" in the hospital. It sucks trying to play Halo on low volume."

Dan said goodbye to Jason and Bobby and then dropped off line as well. Jason sat his controller down and wheeled back towards his bed.

"Do you miss it?" Bobby asked.

"Hmm?" Jason said.

"Going to parties and stuff." Bobby supplied.

Jason shrugged. "A little," he admitted, "but not really."

"Seriously?" Bobby said. He clearly didn't buy it.

"Seriously," Jason said, "I mean being here sucks the big one, no doubt. Honestly though... Dan, he's cool. He's been my best friend for like, ever. The rest of them can go rot for all I care. I mean, I spent like most of my life wanting to be popular or cool or something. Now I am here and suddenly everything they think is cool just seems so lame."

"Like having parties?"

"All they do is drink and congratulate each other on how popular or cool they are," Jason said, "Or make fun of kids who aren't as cool or popular. It pisses me off when I think about it. They'd never give you a chance. The girls would be like, he's sick that's gross. The boys would be 'he's bald let's pick on him'."

"Thanks for the vote of confidence." Bobby said sourly.

"I didn't mean it like that," Jason responded quickly. "You are cool."

"Yeah, right." Bobby responded.

"No, seriously man," Jason said as earnestly as he could, "You are like the coolest kid I've met. Really. Two months ago I would have never stopped to talk to you, let alone taken the time to get to know you. I would have been too worried about what they thought."

Jason thought and went on, "Or Alex, for example. A male nurse? Those guys would laugh. But Alex is like the coolest adult I've ever met. Or Nikki. Nikki is freaking awesome! She is so sweet and caring. I've never met anyone like her."

"Yeah," Bobby agreed, "Nikki is one of a kind."

"She was here this afternoon. While you were gone to your test. How was it by the way?" Jason said realizing that he hadn't asked and Bobby hadn't said.

Bobby shrugged. "Still dying of cancer." Bobby had a dim view of the many tests the doctors wanted to do and what exactly they were all supposed to show. "What did you guys talk about?" Bobby asked.

"My accident actually," Jason said and then wanting to change the subject, "I can talk to Nikki about things I can't seem to say to anyone else. I've never met anyone I am so comfortable with. I really like her."

"Like her?" Bobby asked, putting a peculiar emphasis on the word like.

Jason blushed, suddenly realizing that he did indeed 'like' Nikki but so did Bobby. He tried to think of something, anything to say, "well, I mean, I like her. She's a good friend. I mean, if she wanted more, but she don't. We're friends that's all." He felt like he was babbling.

"Yeah, just friends," Bobby agreed, "Besides you have a girlfriend, right?"

Jason's stomach dropped and he stared blankly at Bobby for a long time. Bobby's eyes narrowed suspiciously and Jason knew he'd revealed something he had not intended.

"You said you had a girlfriend," Bobby said hastily, "that's all."

"Yeah," Jason said, "I have a girlfriend." He turned his chair towards the bed and prepared to transfer himself over. With his back turned he added, "If she's not at the party with someone else by now."

"That's cold, Jason, cold," Bobby said. Jason wasn't sure if Bobby meant his comment or Brittany's actions.

CHAPTER EIGHT

The Second Rule

JASON had learned on his first day in the hospital that the worse the news was, the quieter people talked. Now he was observing Nikki's second rule for being in the hospital. The less a medical professional wants to tell you something, the more they talk. And man this guy was talking.

"Will I ever walk?" Jason asked again.

Dr. Jan hummed to himself. The orthopedic surgeon seemed like a nice enough guy when he spoke English. What he was speaking right now was any one's guess.

"There's been a lot of vascular damage. You can wiggle your toes, which is a good sign.

But there will likely be some nerve deficits..." He continued on in this vein for several minutes before Jason interrupted him again.

"Doctor," he said, "All I want to know is will I walk again?"

"It looks like the bone is healing well." Dr. Jan replied, which was not an answer. "The plastic surgeon was pleased with how the wound in your thigh is healing. The vascular surgeon has even signed off the case."

"Just answer the question," Jason demanded, "Will I walk?"

Seeing no way out, Dr. Jan sighed wearily and removed his glasses. "Honestly it's too early to know. It depends."

"It depends?" Jason echoed, "On what?"

"A lot of things," Dr. Jan answered returning to his litany about vascular damage, nerve deficits, the wound, the shattered tibia and how it was a miracle that they had saved the leg at all.

In the end Jason gave up and listened to the entire litany. When the doctor asked if he had any further questions Jason replied in a sullen voice, "no."

Dr. Jan laid his hand on Jason's arm. "You are healing well." He said encouragingly, "And if I had to guess I would say you are going to get a lot of functionality back. Just be patient."

"A lot of functionality?" Jason thought, "What does that even mean?"

#

The next day Nikki made an appearance

early in the morning, just after breakfast and before Jason went to physical therapy. She said she stopped by to say hi because she was having tests all day and wouldn't be able to come around later.

"Didn't want you guys to miss me, you know." She said.

"What sort of tests are you having?" Jason asked.

She eyed him suspiciously, trying to guess if he was prying for information. (He was.) Then she shrugged and said, "Beth, I mean Dr. Wilson, she's my new endocrinologist, she wants me to take all these tests." Nikki shrugged again, dismissively, "I mean I am stuck here anyway so why not?"

It seemed like a lame reason to do medical tests to Jason. Nikki was gone before Jason had the wit to wonder what an endocrinologist was or why Nikki had one.

When he returned from physical therapy he confronted Bobby. "Look," He said, "I know that you know something about Nikki."

"Yeah," Bobby replied warily, "why do you want to know?"

Jason blew out his breath in frustration. He couldn't explain why it was so important but it was.

"Look," he went on, "I am her friend. I don't mean any harm. I just want to know."

"Know what?" Bobby asked.

"Why is she here? What's wrong with her? Why does she have an endo-whatever it was?

Why-" he broke off. To himself he finished, "why does it say Nicholas on her chart?" He wasn't sure if Bobby knew that or not, and he didn't want to give it away if Bobby was unaware.

It was more frustrating than anything. He would keep Nikki's secrets he had decided, even if her secret was that she was a transsexual. But he couldn't prove to Bobby that he could keep Nikki's secrets because he couldn't tell Bobby about the one he already knew.

"Why is this so important to you?" Bobby demanded. "Just accept it. Nikki will tell you, if and when she's ready."

"I know, it's just," Jason began again.

"This is really bothering you, isn't it?" Bobby asked.

"Yes," Jason whined, "I can't even explain it but it is. I mean you've got this terrible thing happening to you. And we talk about it all the time. I've got this leg, I don't even know if I will ever walk again."

"Is it that bad?" Bobby interrupted suddenly, "I mean I know it's bad, but,"

"I don't really know," Jason admitted, "It's like Nikki says, when they don't want to tell you something they try to talk over your head. All I get is a ton of medical terms I can't understand."

"I'm sorry," Bobby said quietly.

"But that's my point," Jason went on, "They are like that, but we aren't. We talk to each other. You tell me stuff about your cancer and as horrible as it, at least I know. I talk about my leg and it's same. Nikki don't talk. What can possible be so much worse?"

Bobby sighed, "look, it's not a worse sort of thing, it's just private. I wish I could I tell you what I know, but I swore, bro," Bobby looked at him plaintively, "You don't know how serious she was about it."

Jason sighed and let his shoulders droop in defeat. "I don't want you to break an oath man."

#

The next day Bobby's mom came early to meet with his doctors. When they were done she came and got Bobby for a short pass. Nikki was gone again to tests and Jason was left to find something to do by himself. He started a game on the Xbox but was almost immediately bored with it. He thought of getting out his ipad but that seemed to lead him into a morbid mood. His impasse was broken by the sound of many feet coming down the hall and his own name being called.

"Jason!" The voice hooted from the hallway. Jason was sitting up in his wheelchair in front of the Xbox. He craned his neck to see what was going on as the troupe started coming in. Dan was in the lead. Behind was at least half the team. Ron was there and Jeydon even.

"Dude!" Dan said putting his knuckles out against Jason's. "We were like looking forever."

"Yeah," Ron agreed, "this dufus told us the wrong exit." Dan blushed.

"Damn," Roger Corman said, "You fucked your leg!"

Jason looked at his leg. It was propped up as usual. He had gotten so used to seeing the metal hardware sticking out of his lower leg that he almost didn't notice anymore. Now the guys were staring at it in mute horror. Jason shrugged sheepishly.

"Yeah," he said, "They got it pinned in place so it can heal right."

There didn't seem much else to say. The boys spread out. Bobby was out on pass with his mother and several of the boys sat on his empty bed.

"Is?" Dan gestured towards the empty bed, "Cancer boy?"

"Bobby?" Jason asked. "He's out with his mom today." He explained.

"Is he really," Dan's voice dropped to a whisper, "dying?"

Jason shrugged and nodded yes. "Yeah, it sucks. He's really cool."

That stopped the conversation for a while. Ron had a football and kept spinning it in the air in front of him and catching it again.

What did he bring a football for? Jason wondered, did he think they were going to play catch in the hospital?

"That kid next door, the one with the brown hair," somebody asked with a snicker, "is that a boy or girl?"

"That's Nikki," Jason answered angrily, "she's very nice."

There was a hush. When the conversation started up again it was about other subjects. Jason mostly listened. The comment about Nikki, just the tone of the comment, had ruined his mood.

As the conversation progressed his mood did not get better. They talked about football. They talked about the fall line up and prospects, dancing carefully around Jason's departure from the team.

Then Ron started talking about Bingham's party. "Man, I was so wasted, dude!" He told Jason. "It was freaking awesome. You should have been there!"

Jason just glared at him, too angry to answer. Ron didn't even seem to notice Jason's glare. He went right on talking about the party, who was there and how drunk they all got.

"Brittany and Cynthia were like," Ron stumbled comically to show how drunk they were.

"Dude!" Someone hissed.

"What?" Ron said.

Heads nodded in Jason's direction.

"It wasn't nothing," Ron told him dismissively, "she was just blowing off steam. She took your accident really hard, bro."

He wasn't even out of the hospital and she was out partying with her friends? *Yeah, she took it really hard.* He wanted to rage at Ron, to throw something at him and to make him see somehow. Look what I did, he thought savagely, I got in my car drunk and I f-ed up my life forever.

How do you guys react? You drive out to Bingham's farm and get drunk, because you "took it hard"? Are you all idiots?

He wanted to say that but he couldn't. Despite everything some part of him still wanted to be part of that crowd, still wanted to be liked by these guys. He felt torn. Besides, would it really do any good? Would they listen if he told them not to drink again? Probably not. He sighed and his anger turned to sadness.

He shrugged, "Yeah, you know it's our last summer before graduation. If I weren't stuck here I'd be out partying too." He felt sick as he said it, but no one questioned the sincerity of his statement, except maybe Dan who gave him a long hard look.

It was true, part of it anyway. If he hadn't had this accident he would be right there with them, getting trashed on the weekends and hooting and hollering about it all week.

What if his accident had happened to someone else. What if Dan had been maimed? Would that have stopped him? Would he have paused even to consider what had happened?

He thought he would have. It was obvious the majority of the boys had not. They had not stopped for one second to think about what had happened to Jason or how it might happen to them. Were they blind? By the time one of the boys announced that they should get going, Jason was glad to see them leave.

"Don't worry man," Ron said as he clapped Jason on the shoulder, "When you get out of here we'll throw you a huge bash, make up for everything you've missed so far this summer."

Jason merely nodded, not trusting himself to answer.

"I'll come back when I can," Dan said, putting his hand on Jason's shoulder as well. Then, as if he understood, he added, "alone."

CHAPTER NINE

Day of Reckoning

"ALEX?" Jason asked. His palms were sweating and his heart was racing.

Alex seemed to catch Jason's anxiety. "What do you need?" He replied.

"Could you stay and talk a minute? If you're not busy?" Jason asked.

"Sure," Alex responded promptly. "Anything special you want to talk about?"

Jason gestured for Alex to take a seat and Alex complied. "I want to ask you something and I want a straight answer."

Alex nodded. "Okay, shoot."

Jason took a deep breath and said, "Will I ever walk again?"

Alex sighed and looked away. "I was afraid this was coming."

"Will I?" Jason asked again.

"That depends" Alex answered.

"Don't give me a bunch of medical crap," Jason warned.

"I won't." Alex said. "It depends on what you mean by walk."

How many meanings to walk are there? Jason thought irritably. He was silent and let Alex go on.

"Your lower leg is healing great." Alex said, "It will most certainly be able to bear weight. Your ankle is a mess. So is your knee. This," he put a hand near Jason's thigh, "that's muscle tissue that's just gone. With physical therapy, a lot of physical therapy, you can get back some of the mobility and some of the muscle mass, but its never going to be like it was."

"But I will be able to walk?" Jason wanted to know.

"With help, yes." Alex replied.

"Help?" Jason echoed. "What does that mean?"

"Best case scenario?" Alex replied, "A cane. Maybe someday you will be able to do short distances on your own. Worst case scenario would be a walker. Most likely scenario is crutches or some similar device."

"I am going to have to use crutches forever?" Jason asked.

Alex nodded. "I wish I had better news. I

wish I could tell you that you would play ball again, but that's just not in the cards."

"But I will walk," Jason said, "Or hobble at least."

#

"Hey, Brit." Jason said into the phone. He hoped he sounded casual.

"Why are you calling this early?" She asked irritably. He looked at the clock. It was ten thirty am. He had been up, had his leg re-dressed for the hundredth time, been told he would spend the rest of his life hobbling around with a cane and been to physical therapy. She sounded like he'd woke her.

"I just figured I'd try to catch you before work." He answered. Brit had a part time job life guarding at the city pool.

"We don't open until one pm on weekdays." She griped.

"Sorry, I just wanted to talk." He said.

"What about?" She asked shortly.

Suddenly he wasn't so sure he wanted to tell her his news. "I don't know," he answered, "I just wanted to talk. How are you?"

"Umm, fine I guess." She answered.

"How was Bingham's party?" He said. Internally he cursed himself. This was one line of discussion he did not want to have, not now, not ever. Why did his mind always do this to him? He tried to change the subject to avoid one thing he did not want to talk about only to start on another equally bad topic. He had done it the other day with Nikki, admitting to being drunk because he didn't want to talk about her condition. Now he was doing it with Brittany.

"It was okay," she said, "It would have been better if you had been there."

"Yeah, thanks," he replied, "I miss," he paused and considered what he missed. Being able to walk? "I miss everything. I wish I was out there having fun."

"I know." She said, "it really sucks, Jason, what happened to you. It sucks."

"Yeah," he agreed. "How's life guarding this summer?" He asked it mostly because he needed some new topic to discuss.

"It's okay. The pool sucks and Mr. Belaveu is an ass, as always." Mr. Belavue was the city manager, who ran the pool. "Jeydon's head life guard though and he's pretty cool to work for." She finished.

Jeydon, Jason thought wryly, I bet he's cool to work for.

"You guys went out to Oakland Mills, right?" He said. He meant the entire lifeguard team, or so he told himself.

"Who told you that?" She answered suspiciously. His stomach lurched.

"I saw pictures on Facebook," he responded.

"Shit. Jason." She replied, "You call me first thing in the morning to talk about this?"

"Is there going to be a better time?"

She said "Shit" again and then, "Look, what happened to you really sucks. It does. I hate it. I have been totally freaked by the whole thing. It sucks for me too. My boyfriend is in the hospital. You nearly died, in case you didn't know. How am I supposed to feel about that?" It sounded like she was crying on the other end of the line. "There's no one I can talk to. No one understands. I needed to vent, to blow off some steam. Jeydon, he's a great listener. I got too drunk. I didn't mean for it to go so far. I didn't," she finished in a small voice.

"Shit." Jason said into the phone and then he sat the phone in his lap. He couldn't believe she was trying to play on his sympathy in this way. Oh, poor baby, your boyfriend is in the hospital. That must be so stressful for you. Wait a minute, I am the boyfriend. What about me? I am never going to walk right again and you want me to feel sorry because you got drunk and cheated on me?

"Jason," Her voice drifted up meekly to him, "are you still there?"

He looked at the phone in his lap. He looked at his leg, stuck out in front of him. It ached dully, as it often did after therapy even though it hadn't been worked. He should be angry at her, he thought. He should be upset, crying or something. Instead he felt cold, empty and more than a little vindicated. His three-year run as a football stud was over and the saddest part was that not one of those people had proven worthy of even the tiniest bit of the popularity they had.

"Jason?" Her voice was sounding worried.

"I'm here." He said lifting the phone to his ear.

"I'm sorry Jason." She said, "I really didn't mean it to happen. I've just been dealing with so much,"

That did make him angry. "You aren't dealing with shit, Brittany." He snapped. "It's not your leg that got tore up. It's not your life that is ruined."

"I know, you've got it worse by far." She snapped back, "That doesn't mean it's been a picnic for me."

It's not put a cramp in your partying, he thought. Out loud he said, "Let's just stop right here."

"What do you mean?" She asked.

"Stop. Done. I've got too much shit I am dealing with right now anyway. Let's just be over." He said. He wanted to end this call as quickly as possible. He couldn't bear to draw it out any longer.

There was a long pause and then she said, "are you sure?"

"Yeah, I'm sure." He replied, his voice tight.

"I'm sorry, Jason," she said, "I didn't want it to end like this."

#

Jason felt bored and restless. He probably should be crying over Brit or something but he didn't feel that upset, just bored and restless. Bobby was gone yet again for another round of tests. It was like the doctor's devised new MRI and CAT scan studies just for him. Jason sighed. He could play on the Xbox or watch a movie but he didn't really feel like it.

Instead he started rolling himself towards the door. Nikki too was gone much of day lately. Her new endocrinologist, which Jason had learned had something to do with hormone levels, was putting her through a ton of tests. The tests were strange too, especially considering who was prescribing them. She had Nikki see a psychologist. Why would a medical doctor want her to see a shrink? And didn't she already have a shrink?

He saw her wheelchair going into her room as he made for his door. He decided to pay her a visit and followed. It took him a couple of minutes of maneuvering to get out of his door and across the hall. He was getting faster but turning corners with one leg stuck out perpendicular in front of him was no easy task. When he knocked and then rolled into her room she was standing by the edge of her bed, facing away from him. She took a couple of steps to reach for a book.

"You can walk!" Jason said, dumbfounded.

She turned and looked at him quizzically. "Yeah, I can walk." She replied.

"I've never seen you out of your wheelchair." He said sheepishly.

"Oh," she replied then after thinking a minute, "yeah, your probably right. I can walk, I am just not supposed to. Not much anyway.

Outside of the room I am suppose to be in the chair."

She shuffled back down the bedside, being careful of the catheter line that was attached to the bed frame. She sat down and looked at him.

Before he could help himself he blurted it out. "Nikki, why are you here?"

She looked away, her face inscrutable. "I don't like to talk about that." She said.

"I know, but why? Why don't you like to talk about it?" He asked.

"I just don't," she replied.

"Is it so terrible?" He asked.

"It's not, it's just different. Why do you want to know? Does it really matter?" She asked.

"I want to know." He answered but he felt like he needed to know. He couldn't quite say why it was so important, especially right now, but it was. "I want to know the truth."

"Why?" She demanded.

"Because the first day I was here, I was terrified to say anything, even hi, to Bobby. Because," he dropped his voice into an exaggerated whisper, "*he's dying*." He went on in a normal voice, "then you came in and poked him and said 'you dead yet'. It was amazing."

Nikki smiled sheepishly at the description. "Was not," she said.

"It was." He said. "It taught me something I would never have guessed. That one person who was willing to be honest, not quibble or whisper or talk circles around an issue can mean so much. I would have never become friends with Bobby if it wasn't for you."

"You are trying to flatter me." She said, "and you are changing the subject, why do you want to know about me?"

"I am not changing the subject." He insisted. "This morning Alex told me I will always walk with a cane or crutches, I will never be able to walk on my own."

"Never?" Nikki laid her hand on his knee.

"Don't you see?" He said. "Bobby can cope with what he's going through because of you, you are always straight with him even when no one else is. I can make it, no matter how hard it is, because I know Alex is being straight with me. This is it, now I just have to deal."

"Are you sure?" She asked, "That is pretty serious news."

Jason was not about to be pulled off track now. "Listen, Nikki," he put his hand on hers. It felt nice. "Let me be that person for you. Let me be the one that can hear the worse and say, it's okay, we'll get through it somehow."

She looked at him hard. "No," she said, "You don't understand. It's not some terrible thing. I am not dying. It's just," she paused and said, "when I tell people, things change. Things change and they don't go back, ever. It's just different."

"I already know part of it." He said.

"You do?" Her eyebrows arched as she spoke and clearly she did not believe him.

"I know your real name is Nicholas." He said.

She pulled her hand away quickly. She buried her face in her hands and said, "go away."

"Nikki," he said as gently as he could, "If you are transgender, that's okay. I'll still be your friend, I won't judge you."

"I am not transgender." She said through her hands.

He just stared at her. He had thought he had it all worked out. If she wasn't transgender then what?

After a long time she lowered her hands and regarded him. "Fine," she declared, "Nosy. I am intersex."

"inter-what?" He asked. She might as well have been speaking Greek.

"Intersex," Nikki repeatedly slowly. Then she sighed and added, "It's the technical term. The old term was hermaphrodite."

"Hermaphrodite?" He echoed.

"We don't use that term anymore," she told him firmly, "but yeah that's pretty much it."

He continued to stare, dumbfounded. "You are," he trailed off. She sighed.

"I was born with something between my legs that was too big to be classified as girl parts and too small to be called boy parts." She told him bluntly.

He was staring at her in amazement. Out of all the wild guesses he had made this had not once crossed his mind. But as he looked her over it made a sort of sense. She had a flat chest but vaguely feminine body. Her voice was high. If forced to take a stand Jason would have identified her as a prepubescent girl, except she was clearly too old to not have gone through puberty, unless.

"And this is exactly why I don't tell people," she said sarcastically.

"What?" He asked.

"You are looking at me wondering if I am more like a boy or more like a girl. Next you will be stumbling over pronouns, not sure if you should say she or he." She held up the book she had been reading. "Now if I tell you I want a romance novel next you will think, that's a girl trait. If I ask for a fantasy novel you'll think, boy trait. It will all go on some invisible tally sheet in your head."

"No," he said. He forced himself to look up and meet her eyes. He was scared that everything she said was true. He had been wondering if she looked more like a boy or a girl. But he had promised her that he would be the brave one, that it wouldn't matter to him. He met her gaze and saw fear in her eyes. In Nikki's eyes. Those sad brown eyes hadn't changed at least. If he could only hold on to that. He took a deep breath. "That was a doozy," he admitted sheepishly, "but I said I wanted to know."

"You did." She agreed.

"Okay so go on. You were born with something ambiguous down there," He prompted.

"Yeah, ambiguous." She agreed sardonically. "There's a fold but no lady parts. There's something sticking out, but it's not exactly boy parts. They did a DNA test and it came back male." She shrugged, "so my parents named me Nicholas." She looked away and stared off into space for a long while. When she looked back she said, "My parent's took me to some of the top experts. They all said the same thing. Gender is just a cultural thing. Raise the kid as a boy and he'll be a boy. When the time comes we'll do surgery to make him a boy, as best we can."

"For a long time that just how it was, too." She said sadly. "I knew I was different from an early age, how could I not? But I didn't know anything about the diagnosis or anything. At first I was given boy toys and encouraged to do boy things. So I did. It seemed to be working."

"The rules for being Nikki!" Jason exclaimed suddenly.

"Yeah, it worked well, at first. At least when mom and dad were in charge of buying clothes and toys and determining what activities I was allowed to do. But as I got older it got more and more complicated. I seemed to completely lack any internal sense of gender. They tell me blue is for boys and I am a boy so I should wear blue. So one day I go to school in a gorgeous powder blue sweater and everyone laughs. 'That's not a boy sweater' they say. I say 'but it's blue?'"

Jason started laughing. He just couldn't help himself. Nikki kicked his wheelchair playfully. "Are you laughing at me?" She said angrily, but her eyes danced merrily.

"I can just see you in your powder blue sweater," He said meeting her gaze again and smiling.

"And purple," she began indignantly, "That's okay for boys, right?"

"Right," he agreed.

"But lavender, which is a shade of purple is not!?" She went on. She gave him an indignant look but he could see a twinkle in her eye.

They both laughed and he reached for hand again. She let him take it. "You are truly one of a kind," He told her. "So, they instituted the rules for being Nikki?"

"It was a long slow process really," she replied. "They meant well. They were trying to help me get along. I saw Dr. Kinnick even then. My parents would tell him things like, Nick doesn't want another toy truck, he wants a doll and the doctor would say, 'well he must be getting mixed messages. Make him have more play dates with boys his age.' Or 'maybe he needs a rule against dolls'. It just sort of grew and grew. At first I didn't mind so much. When I was six I played with trucks and slept with a teddy bear. By the time I was nine I was sick to death of trucks, and they decided I was too old for a teddy bear."

Jason snickered. "I still have my teddy bear." He said with a smug tone. "I don't sleep with it or anything but mom won't throw Boo-boo away."

She kicked his chair again. "Boo-boo? You named your teddy bear Boob-boo?" She joked.

"I was four when I got Boo-boo." Jason protested.

"Dork," Nikki said. Jason smiled and she smiled back.

"You don't want to be a boy, do you?" He asked.

She again buried her hands in her face. "I've tried to tell them," she said, her voice thick. "I've tried."

A cold sweat broke over Jason as the final piece of the puzzle fell into his lap. He put his hand over his mouth. "Oh my god!" He said. "You said they were going to do surgery, when you were old enough, surgery to make you a boy."

She nodded yes, her face still buried.

"That's what you're here for!" He said.

"They've done it," she said quietly, "they've made me a boy."

CHAPTER TEN

A virgin death

WHEN Jason got back from physical therapy the next morning one of the nurses, Angie greeted him with a cryptic message. "Nikki and Bobby said they needed to go see the open skies, whatever that means." She said with a shrug.

"The outpatient lobby," Jason replied, "Gotcha." He turned around in the hall and headed towards the second floor lobby of the outpatient plaza, where Bobby and Nikki went to pretend they were outside.

Sure enough they were there. Bobby had pulled the bench up close to the railing so he could rest his chin on the top rail and stare blankly out at the overcast sky. Nikki had parked her chair next to him. Her face was down and neither of them seemed to be talking.

"Hey guys," Jason said as he rolled his wheelchair up to them. "What's up?"

"He's in a mope," Nikki said gesturing at Bobby. There was a nervous glint in her eyes as she looked at Jason and then quickly looked away.

"Don't pin it all on me," Bobby said sourly, "You've been moping too." He glanced at Nikki as he said it.

Jason parked next to Bobby. Looking up at the sky he said, "well, I suspect Nikki is in a funk because she's worried that now that I know about her condition I will act all weird around her." He had lain awake long into the night thinking about what Nikki had told him. The only conclusion that he had come to was that Nikki was a good friend and he didn't want to see her hurt anymore than she already had been. "I won't though." He added with a quick reassuring glance. She gave him a wan smile. "So, why are you in a funk?"

"The tests they've been doing," Bobby said slowly, "show more growths."

"What does that mean?" Jason asked.

"The chemo is not working." He replied. "That drug was it. There are no more FDA approved treatments." He shrugged. "The doctors are trying to get approval for some experimental treatments but there isn't much left they can do." Bobby sighed heavily, "I mean I knew the treatment was a long shot and this doesn't really change anything but somehow there's a finality to hearing it."

"Dude, that sucks." Jason said.

"Yeah," Nikki agreed, "Even when you know it's coming, bad news is hard. How are you doing with your news, Jason?"

Bobby looked at him quizzically and Jason realized that he had been so distracted yesterday evening that he hadn't shared his news with Bobby.

"I talked to Alex yesterday," he said, "He says even though the bone will heal enough to bear weight, my knee and ankle are so messed up I'll never walk right. I'll need crutches or something."

"Whoa dude," Bobby said, "that bites. You okay?"

Jason shrugged not trusting himself to speak. After awhile he said, "It sucks but at least I have leg and I will walk."

They stared at the gray clouds. Jason's mood felt as bleak as the sky. Nikki however seemed to have recovered since Jason's reassurance. "Okay, there's only one way out of this funk." She declared after a while.

Bobby shot him a don't ask sort of look. Jason ignored it.

"How?" He asked.

"Mope off." She declared firmly.

"Mope off?"

"It's a contest to see who can complain,

mope or whine the worse." Bobby explained. "She does this whenever one of us is down."

"Every family vacation since I've been eight has been a trip for me to see some specialist somewhere." Nikki said. She looked over at Jason.

"Okay," he said, "Let's see. In middle school I was a complete loser. The only reason I got popular in high school was football. Now I'm not going to have that and I'll probably be a loser again."

"Nice," Nikki said with a nod, "You've got it."

He smiled. It had hurt to say it out loud but it felt good to get it off his chest.

"I was going to go out for football." Bobby said, "I don't know if I would have been any good, but I was going to try."

"Why didn't you?" Jason asked.

"I went in for the physical. The doctor asked me if I knew that I had a bump on my thigh. I didn't. Three weeks later the results came back malignant. Since then I've been kind of busy with the cancer and all that." Bobby explained.

"Ouch!" Jason said.

"Yeah, he's tough at this game," Nikki put in.

"We all have to have one thing we are good at," Bobby said sardonically.

"Okay round two," Nikki said, "I am spending the entire summer stuck in the hospital having a surgery I don't even want."

"I'll never walk right again," Jason said.

"I'm dying." Bobby said with a sigh.

Nikki cursed. "Stop it!" She shouted playfully, slapping Bobby on the back. "You are impossible! You don't even let anyone else score a single point. No! You've got to be the most miserable kid of all time."

A passerby noticed Nikki's outburst and was looking appropriately scandalized. Bobby however was smiling and it was all Jason could do to hold in his laughter.

"Fine," she said, "I don't even know if I am boy or a girl."

Jason thought and said, "I broke up with my girlfriend yesterday."

Nikki gave him a sharp look at the news. Bobby sighed and sat his chin on the rail again.

"You did?" Nikki asked, "Why?"

He didn't really want to get into it. "She only dated me because I was the star running-back. She didn't sign on for any of this. It seemed like the easiest thing for both of us."

"That's cold," Nikki fumed, "to break up with someone in the hospital. That's cold! God you must be so mad!"

Jason shrugged. "Not really," he replied and found it was true. "I've got enough to deal with without her drama."

"Still," Nikki said and settled into a silence.

"I'll probably die a virgin," Bobby said from his seat.

Bobby glanced at Jason. Jason put his

hands up and said, "whoa, I can't help you with that one, bro." Bobby smiled vaguely. He glanced at Nikki.

"I don't even have the right equipment to help you," Nikki protested.

They sat in silence for awhile after this statement but Jason felt it was a more comfortable silence and his funk at least had lifted slightly. On they way back to the unit for lunch Nikki was back to her usual self and raced Jason through one long wide stretch of hall.

After lunch it was Bobby, not Jason, that took a nap. Jason watched him sleep for awhile, wondering whether Bobby's exhaustion was psychological or a dire sign of things to come.

As much to distract himself as anything he pulled out his iPad and got online. He checked his Facebook and found a dozen messages waiting for him. They all amounted to same thing. Brit had changed her Facebook relationship status to single and everyone wanted to know why.

He went to her page and confirmed that she had indeed changed her status. She had also changed her profile picture. Now it showed the lifeguard team at the pool. He couldn't help but notice that she and Jeydon were conspicuously close together. He could almost assume another status change would happen before the summer was over.

He sighed and let it go. He decided he

should at least get back in the conversation a bit. He responded only to Dan's message. He told Dan he had broke it off with Brit and nothing else. Gossips would be having a heyday, he was sure. An online flame war would only add fuel to that fire and since he was likely not going to be part of the A crowd anymore, he would likely to end up the worse off for it.

He changed his status as well. Then he posted a new profile picture. He thought about a bunch of old pictures but in the end choose one of the few newer pictures he had.

Alex had taken it with Jason's iPad at Nikki's insistence. Jason was in the lounge in his wheelchair. He was wearing a loose fitting blue shirt and baggy shorts. The wide bandage across his thigh was clearly visible, as was the metal hardware sticking out of his lower leg.

To his right was Bobby in his stocking cap and a hospital issued bathrobe. He looked pale but happy in the picture. On Jason's left was Nikki. She was in blue hospital scrubs. She had an over-sized book in her hands (she had been reading to some of the younger kids) and she was smiling. She looked for all the world like a girl in the picture.

He titled the picture "chillin on the peds ward." In the course of tagging the picture he discovered that Bobby had a Facebook page and he sent a friend request. Nikki was not on Facebook. He was not surprised. She had said her family was struggling financially and they didn't have a computer at home. Her only Internet access was at school where she was forced to be Nick.

His thoughts were interrupted by Nikki herself, rolling through the doors. She got her wheelchair caught on the end of Jason's bed and the noise woke Bobby.

"Sorry," she said.

"It's okay," he replied tiredly, "I was just dreaming about my afternoon pudding cup anyway." He winked as he said it and she smiled back. She produced the remains of a twelve pack of vanilla and offered them each one and a plastic spoon.

A soft noise from his iPad indicated an incoming message as Nikki rolled back to face them both. It was a message from Dan.

"My friend Dan says he's got permission to borrow the car tomorrow." He told the two of them, "He's coming to visit. It would be cool if you two could meet him."

He answered Dan's message quickly and then he signed off and shut down his iPad. They talked about trivial things for awhile. Pretty soon Bobby faded out again, his pudding cup half eaten.

Nikki turned her attention to Jason. "Are we really cool?" She asked.

"Yeah," he replied. "I mean honestly you are right about a lot of that stuff. It's hard not to think about it all, like you said, not to tally up the masculine and feminine traits." He saw her eyes start to harden and he put his hand on her thigh, "But when I look at your face, you are still the same Nikki. What I am trying to say is, I can see why you hide it. And I am going to do my best to treat you the same. It's the least I can do."

"Thank you," she said in a quiet voice.

"But can I ask you some questions?" He said.

"Like what?" She answered.

"I am not trying to pry or be all pervy, I just," he shrugged, "I guess there's just a big blank spot in my mind around parts of this."

"Blank parts?" She asked.

"Yeah, like how do they do it? How do they make someone a boy? I can't figure it out in my head, it's just a big black circle." He said.

Nikki laughed. "Oh come on use your imagination."

"I can't." He said helplessly, "I am drawing a total blank."

She regarded him levelly "Okay. I'll talk. There are two sides of it, really. One side is hormones. That's the easy part. estrogen for girls, testosterone for boys. I take shots every other week."

Shot day, Jason thought. He kept it to himself.

"Downstairs is another issue." She said. "That's a two stager. The day after school let out I checked into the hospital. My parent's had it all planned out over a year ago, it takes long enough that summer was the only time they could do it and not have me miss a ton of school."

She grimaced and went on, "The first stage was to take a strip of flesh off my thigh and roll it up into a tube, like a penis, sort of."

"They took skin off your thigh?" Jason said aghast.

"Worse," she told him, "they only half took it. They leave it attached on one end."

"Like it's hanging off your leg?" He asked appalled.

"No, one end they left attached to my thigh, the other end of the tube they attached," she pointed to her crotch, "there."

Jason crunched up his nose, trying to get a visual.

"It's like a big U shape." She supplied, "I get to be like that for six weeks. Once the end attached to my crotch heals, they can cut the end attached to my thigh and, voila, I have a penis. Or at least I will have something that looks like a penis. It won't do anything, not that I would want, that." She made a face.

"Damn," he said. "I can't even begin to imagine having something done like that against your will."

"It's not like that," she said shaking her head. "They mean well, my parents." She went on, "this is what all the experts say should be done. They say someday I will be so glad I am a 'normal' male."

"Are you glad?" He asked. She looked away and didn't answer. He sighed and let it go.

"So you have to be in the hospital the whole time?" He asked.

She shrugged, "mostly I guess. They want to monitor me closely. I could have gone to some sort of temporary housing out of the hospital proper, but that would require one of my parent's to stay with me; they don't want me to do much walking or have to do too much for myself while it's healing."

"Your parents wouldn't stay?"

"Couldn't!" She insisted stubbornly, "you don't understand how expensive this is, all of this. They both work so hard." She was suddenly crying, "Dad works two jobs and mom works as much as she can as well. They have both given so much so that I can have a chance at a normal life. Then I am so mean about it sometimes. I should appreciate what they do for me, I know I should."

"But you don't want to be a boy." Jason said.

"I don't, I really don't," She cried even harder. "But they have worked so hard for this, to give me this opportunity. If I tell them how I feel, when I even try, I feel like I have kicked them in the teeth."

Bobby's eyes were open to slits. He regarded them quietly but did not interrupt. Jason had never seen this side of Nikki. She had her face buried in her hands and she was crying harder and harder.

"Nikki!" He said sharply, "You have the

right to be happy too. They may have worked as hard as you say, but that doesn't mean they are right."

Nikki stopped shaking but continued to cry. The nurse Andrea appeared in the doorway.

"Oh dear," she said.

She went to Nikki's side. "We had better get you back to your room if you're upset." She gave Jason a sharp look, like it was his fault that Nikki was upset.

"I am okay," Nikki said meekly. Her hands came down. Her eyes were red from crying. "I just got talking and got upset. I'm sorry. I'll be good."

The nurse would have none of it. She took Nikki's chair and pulled her from the room. Nikki gave them a sad wave good-bye and a mouthed apology as she was pulled from the room.

#

Bobby looked, and felt, better the next day when Jason got back from physical therapy. The two were trying to decide between a movie or Xbox when the phone rang. They exchanged glances. Eleven in the morning was an odd time for either of their parent's to be calling and no one else ever called them.

Bobby picked up the phone and spoke briefly. Then he handed it over to Jason. It was Dan.

"Hey dude," Dan said, "What's up?"

Jason smiled. "Not much, you?"

"Just blew into town. Mom gave me like thirty dollars to get you something but I ain't got a clue. What do you want?" Dan asked.

Jason's stomach rolled and he knew in an instant what he wanted. "Jimmy Johns." He said.

"Jimmy Johns?" Dan echoed.

"Yup," Jason said. He held his palm to the receiver and said to Bobby, "Go ask Nikki what she wants. My treat." Bobby smiled and disappeared.

"Mom found one in Coralville, not far from the hospital exit." He told Dan.

"Yeah," Dan said. "I just passed it. Hold on I'm turning back."

"No problem," Jason said, "I sent Bobby to get Nikki's order." Jason waited, not wanting to distract Dan with too much conversation while he was driving. Pretty soon Bobby was back with Nikki's order and Jason was relaying all three orders to Dan.

"Are you sure this is what you want me to do with the money?" Dan asked one last time.

"After weeks of hospital food?" Jason replied, "You bet."

Nikki appeared, rolled into the room by a nurse, Angie. Jason sighed and thought, "I am glad it's Mcbitch's day off."

"What's this I hear?" Angie said in mock anger, "You guys don't like our wonderful hospital cooking?"

Less than a half an hour later Dan was

there, carrying a Jimmy Johns box and a disposable tray of drinks. Jason greeted him and introduced his new hospital friends to his best friend.

"Cancer boy!" Dan said when introduced to Bobby. "Man, you smoke butt on Xbox live."

"Thanks," Bobby replied sheepishly.

"Is it true that all you guys do is play Xbox all day?" Dan asked as he handed over a sandwich.

"No," Bobby replied sarcastically, "sometimes we watch movies."

"Some of us read," Nikki said with equal sarcasm.

"If they let me out of school," Dan said. "There's no way you'd catch me reading." He shuddered.

Jason smiled and held up a book. "Nikki's got me reading this. It's not bad. So apparently you can teach an old dog new tricks."

Dan passed Nikki her sandwich and then Jason his. He retrieved the final sandwich from the box and sat on Jason's bed to eat. Jason backed his wheel chair against the wall by the head of the beds, and Nikki backed hers against the opposite wall by the foot of the beds, so they formed a diamond where they could all see each other.

Dan and Bobby immediately struck up a conversation about Xbox live, the games they both played and the online players they knew. Jason worried that Nikki would get bored with all of the game talk but as the day progressed into afternoon Nikki and Dan found they had a rather strange common ground. Dan loved movies, especially sci-fi and fantasy movies. Nikki loved reading, especially sci-fi and fantasy. Most of the movies that Dan loved, Nikki had read the books. They talked about Harry Potter, Lord of the Rings and one Nikki had not gotten to see yet, the Hunger Games.

Around mid afternoon Nikki let Angie know she wanted to "call in a favor." She resolutely refused to tell the boys what this cryptic remark meant, but around three thirty, after Angie went off shift the nurse returned with four chocolate shakes from the cafeteria.

Jason was glad to see that his best friend at least could get along with his hospital friends. He was also glad that Dan wasn't over cautious around Bobby or over inquisitive about Nikki. He just accepted them the way they were.

Just when Jason was starting to feel down because he was sure that Dan would have to leave soon, Bobby sighed dramatically and said, "well, I guess supper is my turn. I am sorry but it won't be as good as lunch or the malts." His malt sat barely touched on the bedside table as he rummaged through one of the drawers but he seemed in good spirits. He came out with a small hospital voucher. He handed it to Dan. "This will get you a meal from the cafeteria. I'll have one of the aides open a conference room so we can all have supper together."

"Awesome!" Dan said holding up the ticket. The funny thing was that Dan was obviously being sincere with his remark. He disappeared down the hall while Nikki and Jason maneuvered their chairs towards the conference room.

He was back by the time they had been served their meals. He was positively glowing with excitement as he told them about his trip to the cafeteria.

"Look!" He said, "Turkey loaf, mash potatoes and gravy! And a brownie!" He gestured at his plate, "It's like Thanksgiving, but in the middle of summer! You guys eat like this all the time?"

Nikki stifled a laugh. Bobby answered, "Yeah it's great the first time, but every other Thursday for the last two months, gah."

"Are you kidding? I could eat this every day." Dan gushed.

"No, you couldn't," Jason told him. "Trust me on that."

Dan's mom texted him during supper, wondering where he was and if he'd be home before dark. He texted back and promised he'd leave right after they ate.

As they rolled down the hall towards the exit, and their respective rooms Dan said, "This has been the best day of the summer so far."

"Visiting a friend in the hospital?" Nikki said skeptically.

"Visiting my *best* friend in the hospital." Dan corrected her, "and meeting you two. You guys rock!"

"Thanks," Nikki and Bobby answered together and they both blushed.

"I can not thank you enough," Jason told him extending his hand to Dan.

Dan took it and said, "Better in the hospital with a true friend than anywhere else without you dude."

"You to." Jason replied.

#

The next morning Alex came into his room while Bobby was out. "I've got news," he said, leaning against the foot of the bed.

"News?" Jason asked.

"Yup," Alex said. There was something out of place in Alex's voice but Jason couldn't quite place what. "A room has opened up down the hall." He paused. "A private room." He paused again. Jason just stared at him blankly. "We can transfer you there anytime you want." Alex said.

Jason glanced over at Bobby's empty bed. He looked back at Alex. "Do I have to?"

Alex sort of shrugged. "You know he's..."

"Dying?" Jason finished. "Yes. I still don't want to move. He's my friend."

Alex was suddenly grinning from ear to ear. "You could always refuse," He said.

"I can?" Jason answered and then quickly added, "I do, I refuse to move."

Alex hit the bed playfully, "I knew it.

You're a good egg, Jason." Jason understood suddenly that Alex hadn't wanted to separate him and Bobby, but someone was forcing him to make the offer. He also understood that he had passed some sort of test with Alex, though he wasn't quite sure what the test was. All he knew is that he had no intention of bailing on Bobby now. Besides Bobby and Nikki kept him sane. What would he do all the way down the hall from them?

CHAPTER ELEVEN

Old Glories

THE next day when Jason got back from physical therapy he found Bobby getting ready to leave on pass with his mother. They would go down into Iowa City for lunch and do a little shopping. Bobby's needs were pretty minimal. He needed a couple of new shirts. He was also hoping his mom might spring for a new game for him and Jason to play and possibly even a book for Nikki. Jason wished him well. Not wanting to spend the entire day alone he went looking for Nikki.

He found her in the patient lounge. She had parked her wheelchair beside one of the couches in the far corner and moved over to the couch.

Curled up next to her was Alexis. Jason had met the young girl once before. She was seven and having her first round of chemo for Leukemia. Already her beautiful blond hair was looking patchy and she would have it cut that weekend.

Nikki had an over-sized book in her hands and was reading to Alexis. Jason glided over to them. "What are you girls reading?" He asked.

"If You Give a Mouse a Cookie," Alexis answered.

"Good book," Jason told her. To Nikki he said, "go on." He was not about to compete with a seven year old over Nikki's attention. Besides listening to Nikki read was as good of relief from boredom as anything.

Nikki finished the book and Alexis ran to find another.

"So no video games this morning?" Nikki asked.

"Nope," Jason answered, "Bobby went into town with his mom. I was bored so I came out here."

"Want to go do something?" Nikki asked.

"This is fine," He replied.

Alexis reappeared with another book. Nikki gave him a quizzical look.

"Dr. Seuss," Jason said to Alexis, "You've got good taste in books."

Alexis shot him a look that said, don't I know it? She said, "You can listen too if you want, if it's okay with Nikki."

"Is it okay?" He asked Nikki with a wink.

"Dork," she muttered but she smiled as she said it. Out loud she said, "sure."

He smiled too. He liked it when she called him a dork. She never put that degrading tone behind it and he knew she considered herself one as well. He would much rather be a dork and hang out with kids like Nikki and Bobby then go back to trying to be acceptable to the "perfect" girls in the A crowd, he decided.

He saw a figure in his peripheral vision. It was a man in a tweed suit. The man was sitting down in the lounge chair next to the couch. As he turned he saw the familiar dirty brown hair and pinched face, it was Nikki's father. Under his tweed jacket was a white dress shirt and a thick protruding belly. He looked exhausted and Jason thought about what Nikki had said the other day, how he had to work two jobs to pay for all of Nikki's medical bills.

Jason's mom had let it slip in a phone conversation that the first of Jason's medical bills were arriving. Even with insurance the family's co-pay was enormous and this was going to stress the family budget for a long time to come. He wondered guiltily if his own father would look this exhausted in the months ahead.

"I had a day off." Nikki's father was saying to her, "I thought I should come. I have not seen you in awhile."

Nikki nodded and started to hand the

book back to Alexis but her dad waved her off. "Finish, please." He said.

She nodded and then said, "Dad, this is Alexis and that is Jason. Alexis, Jason, this is my father."

Nikki's father nodded at Alexis and then extended his hand to Jason. "It's Larry," he said.

"Mr. Pagan," Jason said nervously, "umm, Larry." They shook hands.

Nikki began to read again and Mr. Pagan pulled the sports page out of nearby newspaper and began to read to himself. As Nikki's book wound down Mr. Pagan looked over his paper and commented, "Red Sox played a fair game the other day, I caught most of it at the hotel." Mr. Pagan worked as a hotel manager and moonlighted at convenience store.

"Yeah," Jason replied, "we watched it here. It was a very good game."

"We?" Larry asked.

"Yeah, Bobby and Nikki and I," Jason answered. Larry gave a glance at Nikki, his eyebrows arched. "Well," Jason went on, "she, I mean Nikki, mostly read."

Mr. Pagan made a humph noise. Nikki gave Jason an inscrutable look.

"One more book!" Alexis pleaded. Nikki looked at her father who nodded his approval. Alexis dashed off after another book.

"I hear the Vikings picked up Alberts in the first round draft." He commented to Jason.

"Oh yeah," Jason replied, "He's a great lineman. That's always been the Vikings' weakness." Alberts was an offensive lineman for the University of Iowa's football team. He had been picked up on the NFL draft.

Jason and Mr. Pagan discussed the deal, and the Vikings' chances in the fall season while Nikki read to Alexis. When the book was finished Alexis asked for yet another book and Nikki turned her down sharply. "I need to spend some time with my dad." She said. She gave Jason a dark look while she got back into her wheelchair.

"It was good to meet you," Mr. Pagan said, oblivious to the look. "I am glad that Nick has met some friends. I hope your recovery goes well."

To Nikki he said, "I was thinking we could get some lunch in the cafeteria and then maybe I could push you outside, out by the fountain."

"That sounds great." Nikki replied her voice flat.

After Nikki and her dad left Jason offered to read the next book to Alexis. He was not nearly as good at it as Nikki had been and Alexis was not above telling him so. Still they got through it and she thanked him when they were done.

Lunch came and after he had eaten Jason played on the Xbox by himself. He kept the sound down low and sat near the TV. Or at least he pretended that he sat near the TV so he could keep the volume low and not disturb the other patients. Truth be told he was watching the hallway as much as the screen, waiting for Nikki to return.

She was mad at him. He had no doubts about that. Like an imbecile he had said 'Nikki' to her dad, not 'Nick'. He had even said 'she'. He wasn't sure if Mr. Pagan had heard or noticed but Nikki had.

He had screwed up. She had been breaking 'the rules for being Nikki' and now she was found out because of him. He wondered if Mr. Pagan was yelling at Nikki right now. Would she be punished? How?

It was mid afternoon before they returned and Jason was in a state of near panic by that time. He saw them go past, Nikki pushing the door open so her dad could wheel her in. He could hear her dad's voice saying good-bye and could hear them both exchange a perfunctorily "I love you." "I love you too, Dad."

When he was sure her dad was gone around the corner and off the unit he made for her room. He nearly crashed into a cart as he exited the room. It was Alexis.

"Where are you off to?" He called out.

"Tests," she called back. She waved goodbye and was gone.

It was always tests, X-rays, MRI's, CAT scans, you name it. The kids on this ward had more tests than any school kid could ever imagine, Jason thought wearily as he made his way across the hall.

"I am so sorry," he said as he wheeled into Nikki's room.

She was sitting on the edge of her bed. She looked up at him sharply, "What are you sorry about?" She asked irritably.

"I am sorry I called you Nikki," he replied, "did you get into trouble?"

Her eyes scrunched up as she considered that. "No," she replied, "Why?"

He was confused. "But I thought you were supposed to be going by Nick." He said, "Isn't that why you are mad at me?"

"No," she replied, "Why do you think I am mad at you?"

He just stared at her blankly.

"Fine!" She spat out, "I'm mad at you. Happy?" She folded her arms across her chest and regarded him darkly.

"Why?" He persisted.

"Why!" She said in exasperation. "Why do you think?" Since it was obvious he had no clue she went on, "You had to talk about football, didn't you? Big football hero has to go talk sports to my dad."

"And that's bad because?" He asked.

She didn't answer for a long time. When she did she started with a question, "What's the most important thing to a little kid?"

Jason thought about what had mattered to him when he was little, his toys, his playstation. He didn't think that was the sort of thing Nikki had in mind. He shrugged helplessly. "I don't know."

"Approval." Nikki supplied. "Approval from a parent, maybe?" A tear slid down her cheek. "And do you have any idea how often I get that? Little, I-can't-ever-seem-to-do-the-right-thing-without-being-told-a-hundred-times Nikki? Not very often."

"Then along comes Mr. Jock Jason," she went on not looking at him. "My dad makes one comment about sports and you know the answer. Five minutes later you have a better relationship with him then I do."

"How is that my fault?" He answered, hurt. "I was trying to be nice because he's your dad. Am I a terrible person for that?"

"No," she replied sullenly, "It just hurt, to see you two get along so easily, to know that you are the kind of son he wishes he had."

"Well if he can't see what a wonderful child he has, then I don't even like him," Jason responded. He spun his wheelchair around and left the room.

#

Jason paused the video clip. With his finger he ran the bar back about thirty seconds and watched the play again. They were playing Keokuk. It was one the early games last fall. He watched himself feint to the right, down the offensive line. Five steps and about face, he was running back towards the quarterback. The defensive ends had bought the ruse and were fading back to cover the receivers. The quarterback stepped forward and handed him the ball. He took it through the widening hole in the center. The line closed around him but he leaped forward and made a precious few yards.

That was his secret. Others thought that the secret to being a great running-back was to stay on your feet at all cost. Not Jason, as soon as someone laid a hand on him he lunged forward landing a yard or two further down the field. Those extra one or two yards added up. They had gotten his team a first down more times than he could count. They slowly added to his season totals. They got him noticed. In his sophomore year Jose, the first string running-back had scored more touchdowns but by the season's end Jason had more yards gained. Next year Jason was the first string.

He stopped the video and ran the bar back again. He wasn't sure what had prompted him to torture himself in this way. He couldn't help himself. He watched play after play. He didn't watch a single game all the way through. He spotted plays he remembered and watched them over and over.

He glanced at the doorway to his room and then back to the iPad. He knew part of the reason he was torturing himself. It was Nikki. She had no idea what the conversation with her dad had meant for him. He had been trying to be nice, trying to be get on her dad's good side because he was Nikki's dad. Even if that meant talking football.

They had talked about the draft, the draft

that Jason had hoped one day to be part of. He had wanted it so bad he could taste it. Now it would never happen.

Nikki thought he didn't know about approval, that he had never struggled for it. She couldn't be more wrong. He knew. He knew what it was like to work everyday to stay in shape so he could be on the team. He knew what it was like to throw himself through a ragged hole of men, arms reaching out to slam him to the ground, again and again, to win approval, to convince people he mattered. It was the only thing he'd ever been really good at it and now it was gone.

He knew he should be trying to do something to stop the funk, but he couldn't. Besides he had already been on Facebook and that was no better, seeing pictures of all the other kids getting on with their summer, living their lives.

His funk was finally interrupted by Bobby's return. His mother was at his side and they had brought a pizza to share with him for supper. Bobby left to go get Nikki.

"You okay?" Bobby's mother asked him.

"Yeah," he lied, "It's just boring in here sometimes."

"I can imagine," she replied. "Have you had many visitors?"

He shrugged, "My aunt gets up here three or four times a week. Mom would like to come more but it's an hour drive."

She nodded knowingly, "What about your

friends? Bobby tells me one of them came the other day and stayed a long time."

Jason smiled at the memory, "Yeah, that was my best friend Dan. He'd come more but he don't have his own car and his mom works a lot."

"You have a girlfriend?" She asked.

"No," he said quickly.

"Well, I am going to take the next few weeks off and I'll be staying in Iowa City now that," She stopped cold and then went on, "If you need anything, just let me know. I'll make sure you have my cell phone number."

He nodded and thanked her.

Nikki rolled through door and gave Jason a wan sheepish smile. From the doorway Bobby said. "Mom, can we get some cokes from the vending machine?"

"Yeah, sure." She replied grabbing her purse. She followed Bobby out of the room again.

When they were both gone Nikki coughed nervously and said. "It's probably just as well, I think we should talk."

"Okay," he replied hesitantly.

"I'm sorry," she said suddenly, "I shouldn't have gotten mad at you. My dad just drives me so crazy sometimes. I know he really wanted a son."

"He thinks he has a son." Jason said, "but can't he see that's crazy? You are great the way you are."

"Thanks," she said quietly, "but it's a lot

more complicated than that. He's always wanted a son and he's been told by the doctors for years that all he had to do was to raise me to be that son, that I'd accept it eventually." She was on the verge of tears again, "I feel like it's my fault, it's some defect in me that I can't accept what everyone else thinks is right for me."

"That's not true." He said staunchly.

Bobby and his mother returned, stopping their conversation. "I'm sorry too," He whispered quietly as Bobby handed them each a can of Coke. Bobby gave them a quizzical look which Nikki returned with a look that said, "we'll explain later." Jason's stomach grumbled and he was glad to put the fight behind them and concentrate on pizza.

CHAPTER TWELVE

A not so academic debate

THE next day it was Jason's turn to go on pass. His mom arrived early and then had to wait while he went to physical therapy for the day. When he got back he said goodbye to Bobby. Being stuck in a wheelchair he couldn't go off the hospital grounds, but they made the best of it.

They had lunch in the cafeteria and then mom took him out the back entrance of the hospital and to a small park nearby. She had brought him a couple of presents, "just because". The first was a game for Bobby's Xbox and the other was a new shirt. His needs and wants were pretty reduced too and it was good enough.

By late afternoon his mom had to go. She had a meeting in the evening. She promised she'd be back in two days, when the Orthopedic doctor wanted to do another procedure on his leg.

His room was empty when they got back. Jason went to find Bobby and presumably Nikki as well. His nurse did not know where they had went.

He went to the main lobby, and then to the outpatient lobby. He went to a couple of other places as well but they weren't in any of their usual hang-outs. He finally gave up and headed back to the unit. At the entrance to the ward he noticed that one of the conference room doors was ajar. He pushed it open.

Bobby was sitting on one of the couches. His head was back and his eyes were closed. For a moment Jason wondered if he was in pain. Then he noticed there was a dirty reddish-brown mop of hair in his lap and Nikki's wheelchair parked nearby. Bobby was apparently not going to die a virgin after all, at least not completely a virgin.

Jason rolled his chair back quickly and tried to leave before either of them noticed him. His foot hit the door and Bobby's eyes snapped open. Jason rolled away as fast as he could, but out of the corner of his eye he caught Bobby's gaze.

He rolled himself quickly to his room and transferred into the bed. His eyes stung and his mind burned with what he had seen. It wasn't fair, he told himself. He had no right to feel this way. He and Nikki were friends, nothing more. Besides Bobby was dying. He couldn't steal a girl from a dying friend, he wouldn't. It wasn't fair that his heart hurt so much at the thought of Bobby and Nikki together.

The aide had brought in the boys' supper before Bobby returned. Bobby came back a few minutes later. He took a quick nervous glance around the room. Then he put his head down and he walked quickly to his bed.

"Did you have a good time with your mother?" Bobby asked casually, still not looking at Jason. He pulled the bedside table over and inspected his supper. He did not eat.

"Yeah," Jason replied keeping his gaze on his plate. "You have an okay afternoon?"

"Yeah." Bobby replied.

There was a long awkward silence while the two boys picked at their meals, neither eating. Finally, still looking away, Bobby said. "You know when I am dead, she's yours."

"I don't want," Jason replied irritably and broke off.

"Don't want her?" Bobby said, "I don't believe that."

"No," Jason interrupted not denying how he felt about Nikki, "I don't want her like that, I don't,"

"Don't want leftovers?" Bobby said angrily.

"No," Jason said again, "I don't want," he struggled for a breath and then before Bobby could make another assumption he spat it out, "I don't want you to die."

Bobby laughed dryly. "I am not thrilled about the prospect either."

"I know," Jason said, "this whole situation, you, me, Nikki, it sucks. I like Nikki, but I don't want it all twisted up with your dying."

Bobby sighed, "I'm sorry, I didn't mean it like that." He paused and then said, "what I meant was, Nikki is special. In here she keeps us sane. She's strong and brave. But outside of this place she's," he shrugged searching for the word, "fragile. She needs someone. I wish I could be that someone for her, god knows I do. But I can't. Just promise me you'll look after her, help her, whatever that means." He finished.

Jason paused. "Yeah, of course."

There was another long pause while the boys ate, but it was for Jason less awkward. He felt a weight lift off his chest. It wasn't a contest to see who 'got' Nikki. It was a mutual understanding that she was someone special, someone who deserved to be cared for. And part of that specialness was that she would not deny a dying friend his last wish.

#

Bobby was sitting up in his bed when Jason returned from physical therapy in the morning. He looked across the hall at Nikki's closed door and said, "It was shot day. They came and did it while you were away."

"Crap," Jason muttered. He stared at the door as well. "You know," he said finally, "she would come cheer either of us up if we had anything bad to go through."

"She would," Bobby agreed. "You think we should?"

"Yeah, I do." Jason said.

Bobby rose and started towards the door. He stopped and looked back. "She doesn't know, by the way." He said, "that you saw us, I mean."

"She won't find out from me." Jason said quickly. Bobby nodded and turned back towards the hallway. Jason followed him in his wheelchair.

"Hey Nikki," Bobby said as he opened the door, "Thought we'd visit you for a change."

She was sitting on her bed reading from a thick hardcover book. She looked up and regarded them levelly. She seemed upset, but not at them.

Jason coasted in as Bobby sat at the end of the bed. Bobby reached out and touched her hand. She looked uneasily towards Jason but did not pull her hand away.

Jason smiled, trying to show her he was not upset by her and Bobby. He wasn't sure if he succeeded or not. "What'cha reading?" He asked, mostly for some subject to discuss, to ease his growing discomfort.

She held the book up. The title read

"Gender: Biology or Culture?"

"A little light reading?" Bobby said sarcastically.

"Beth, I mean Dr. Wilson, gave it to me." Nikki said.

"It looks like a college textbook to me." Jason said, frowning.

"It is," Nikki said. "Its a bunch of different experts writing different chapters, debating how much of our gender differences are rooted in biology and how much are just cultural conditioning."

"Hmm," Bobby said, "Yeah a lot of fifteen year old girls like to have academic debates about gender."

Nikki slammed the book shut and glared at him. "It's not an academic debate to me!" She snapped.

"I'm sorry," Bobby said hastily.

"It's not you," Nikki said looking away. "It's just this whole book." She gestured around them, "and this place."

"I am not sure I know what that even means," Jason admitted, looking at the book's title again.

"They are debating how much of our gender, whether we perceive ourselves to be male or female and how we behave, is innate, biological tendencies and how much is our upbringing." Nikki explained, "For example everyone knows that men and women tend to have different communication styles. Is that because our brains are different, or because we are raised different?"

"I don't know," Jason said, "Which is it?"

"No one really knows for sure." Nikki said, "for one thing there are a lot of individual differences, not all men communicate the same, nor do all women. And our brains are different too, but the differences are so small that some experts say they don't matter."

"Does it say anything about your condition?" Bobby asked.

Nikki made an irritated noise. "Basically, I am screwed." She said. "If gender is just culture, just how you are raised, then when they told me I was a boy that should have been good enough. I should have been happy as a boy. If gender is biology, then my DNA is male so..."

"Well, then neither of them is right," Jason said, "Cause you want to be a girl."

"It's not that simple," Nikki said. "There are dozens of subtle little things in the brain and subtle differences between boys and girls. It's not all down to what's between the legs. Beth has been having me do all these tests. I've had an MRI of my brain. This tiny little piece is 2 millimeters smaller than the average male but 1 millimeter larger than the average female. So what does that mean?" She threw her hands up in exasperation. "Who knows? I've taken a half dozen psychological tests as well. But it's the same dilemma. I have the visual spatial skills of a boy but the verbal aptitude of a girl. What does that mean?"

"It means you're super smart," Jason answered. She scowled at him. "And you don't even need a test," Jason said to Bobby, "all you have to do is hear her say 'verbal aptitude' in a sentence."

Bobby snorted. "Or see her reading a college textbook." He added.

Nikki threw her pillow at Jason. It hit him in the face and fell on his lap. She leaned over and retrieved it and then hit Bobby with it as well. "This is serious guys," she said. But she smiled as she said it.

She leaned back on the bed, using her pillow to prop her up. "I am just so sick of experts trying to tell who or what I am." She said

Bobby put a hand on her knee. "That would be hard," he said. She gave a short nervous glance towards Jason.

"I thought I had it bad with people expecting things of me because of football. I can't imagine what it would be like to have someone tell me I had to be a girl." Jason laughed.

"You'd make one ugly girl, bro," Bobby joked, still rubbing Nikki's knee.

"What!?" Jason replied in mock astonishment, "You don't think I'd be beautiful as Jasonette." Jason posed in what he thought was a feminine way and called out in a high falsetto, "Hi, I'm Jasonette, don't I look beautiful?" Both Nikki and Bobby lost it while Jason went on in a falsetto about how beautiful he was and how much fun he was having.

"Jasonette's" show was interrupted by a knock on the door. He blushed as he looked and discovered Dr. Jensen, his orthopedic surgeon, standing in the doorway.

"I heard I might find you over here." He said without any introduction, "Am I interrupting?"

"No," Jason said hastily, "I was just kidding around." He blushed heavily again. Dr. Jensen scowled slightly, as though he didn't get the joke. Jason went on, "Umm, you need me to come back to my room?"

"No, no," The doctor replied. "I just wanted to check in quick and see if you understood what was happening tomorrow?"

"Yeah," Jason replied, "You're going to take the metal out of my leg, right?"

"Well, not all of it." Dr. Jensen replied in his usual roundabout way. "We are going to take the hardware out. That's these two pieces here," He gestured at the metal bars sticking out Jason's lower leg. "and the cross pieces. You have a rod inside as well, and that stays."

"For how long?" Nikki asked.

Dr. Jensen glanced at her for moment, as if unsure he should answer. Just when Jason was expecting yet another lecture on confidentiality (the pat answer they gave when one of the kids asked about another kid) the doctor shrugged and said, "Forever."

"Forever?" Jason asked.

"The bone will heal over it," the doctor

explained, "and you'll never have any problems with it. We'll give you a card, like an id, to carry. Your leg will most likely set off metal detectors."

"Cool," Bobby said, "You're like the bionic man or something."

Dr. Jensen scowled again and asked if Jason had any other questions. Jason told him no.

"Is your family going to be here?" He asked.

Jason nodded yes. "My mom, she's coming in tonight and staying with my aunt. They'll both be here."

"Okay then, I will see you tomorrow." The doctor said, "and remember nothing to eat or drink after midnight."

"Got it." Jason said.

After lunch the three of them hung out like normal. Except, Jason kept reminding himself, it was not like normal. It was shot day and they had gotten Nikki cheered up and out of her room. That hadn't happened once since he had been admitted. He was proud of this fact.

His mom showed up around supper time and offered to buy Jason and his friends Jimmy Johns again.

The evening passed quickly, the night even more so. He was woken around midnight by a nurse's aide. She stole his ice pitcher and reminded him sternly he was not to eat or drink anything. "I wouldn't have," He groused to himself, "and if she hadn't woke me, I wouldn't have been thirsty either. I would have just slept through until morning."

Jason didn't sleep through till morning. The hospital ran on it's own schedule and he was woken again about four am. They needed to draw some blood tests, the aide told him this time. Sleepily, he held out his arm for the laboratory lady. Then it was the nurse. She had to start an IV. Jason hadn't needed an IV for several weeks now, but with his procedure today they would once again stick a needle in his arm.

Then about six am the nurse was back, to "finish the checklist" whatever that meant. Finally, not long before seven am, a transporter showed up with a cart. His mom and Aunt Mandy arrived as he was scooting himself over onto the cart. They both gave him a hug as he got ready to leave the room.

"Good luck Mr. Bionic Man," Bobby said sleepily from his side of the room.

"Thanks," Jason replied with a smile, "See you later."

As they turned out in the hallway he found Nikki sitting in her doorway in her wheelchair. She looked wide awake. "Good luck, Jason," she said with a smile and wave.

He turned in the cart to wave back at her. "Thanks, Nikki," he responded.

"She's sure something," his mom said with a knowing look.

"Yeah," he replied, not sure how to even

begin explaining Nikki to his mom.

The surgery waiting room was a lot of hurry up and wait. They bustled him into a space surrounded by curtains. A nurse hurried in, took his vitals, marked something on a clipboard and hurried out. He waited for what seemed like a long time. Then she was back and made Jason shimmy out of his shorts and T-shirt and gave him a hospital gown to wear instead. Finally they ordered his mom out into the waiting room.

Jason sat alone in his little curtained prison for what seemed like forever. Just when he thought he would wait all day they were pushing him through the double swinging doors into the surgery suite.

For Jason, at least, the procedure was as fast as the wait had been long. He recalled the anesthesiologist introducing himself to Jason and pushing something in his IV line. Then he was waking in the recovery room.

Once he was fully awake they let his mom in. He made her lift the sheet around his lower leg and was surprised to find no bandages at all, merely four round nail sized holes in his leg, two on either side and each bearing a single stitch holding it fast together. Apparently that was enough as there was no indication of bleeding at any of the holes.

CHAPTER THIRTEEN

Walking, sort of

"OKAY," Alex said joking, "I want to see you do a triple gainer, a back flip and then dismount, got that?"

Jason stared down the narrow passage created by the handlebars in front of him. He swallowed hard.

"Don't listen to him." Greg, the physical therapist, said at Jason's other side. He was wrapping a wide nylon belt around Jason's waist. "We call this a gait belt," he said, "it's there so Alex and I can grab you if we need to."

It was not everyday that Alex came down to physical therapy, in fact this was the first time Jason had seen it happen. But then again it wasn't every day that your patient walked for the first time either.

"All I am hoping for today," Greg told him seriously, "is to see you stand. If we get that, I'm happy."

Jason nodded. He looked down the passage again. On the far end sat Nikki and Bobby. His mom was standing to one side, her phone out and undoubtedly, the camera on and ready.

Since the hardware had come out Jason had found he could move his leg. It still felt rubbery and numb, like it had fallen asleep. Like so many things, his orthopedic doctor could not tell him if that numbness would ever go away or not.

What movements he could make were crude and hard to control, but it moved nonetheless. Dr. Jensen felt that the bone had healed well and should be able to bear weight. Whether or not the muscles, knee or ankle were up to it was anyone's guess. Greg was eager to test the leg, to find out where they stood. Jason was eager too, but afraid as well.

He took a deep breath and said, "Let's do this."

"Okay," Greg said with a glance at Alex. To Jason he said, "What I want you to do is to grab onto these handle bars and pull yourself up into standing. Keep all your weight on your hands. That's it for the moment, okay?"

"Okay," Jason replied. He grabbed the

handle bars and heaved himself up. He swayed dizzily for a moment. His arms strained at the sudden effort but he held on.

Greg checked Jason's position carefully. With one foot he nudged Jason's right foot forward an inch or two. "There," he said, "now it's squarely under you. Alright, slowly now, lower yourself onto your feet. Don't try to bear all the weight on your leg just yet, just a little bit at a time."

Jason nodded. His mom was holding the phone up taking a picture. Nikki and Bobby were clapping.

Jason felt beads of sweat on his forehead. It was hard to imagine that this was so much hard work, but he knew his body was straining. His left leg felt solid and good. The right was still numb but it seemed to be holding him up. He felt a rush of exultation.

"F- the doctors" he thought savagely, "Fuck them and their predictions, I am going to walk. I am going to fucking walk."

"Good, good," Alex was saying on his left.

"Let's shift your weight to the left leg," Greg was saying. Jason did as he was told.

"Can you move your right leg?" Greg asked.

"You bet I can," Jason said with grim determination. His right foot rose off the ground. It swung forward and then back behind him. He cussed quietly. Finally he got it in front of him again and planted it. He started to lean forward into the step. There was a sharp pain and he fell forward. He would have hit the bar if Alex and Greg hadn't caught him.

"It's okay we got you," Alex said in his ear.

Slowly and painfully he pushed himself upright again. His excitement quickly faded and then turned to despair. He was sweating profusely, just staying upright between the bars was almost more than he could do. Greg coached him calmly and patiently. He was to hold himself upright between the bars and merely put his legs through the motions of walking, without any real weight on them. It didn't matter. No matter how little the weight, the knee gave out. No matter how he willed it the leg swung erratically like Frankenstein's limb.

"I am so sorry." He whimpered as they finally had him sit back in his wheelchair. "I am so sorry."

"Don't be," Alex said though Jason thought he was hiding his disappointment as well, "You did your best."

"I told you," Greg reminded him sternly, "that if you stood, that would be enough for today. You stood."

"I wanted to walk so bad," Jason said in a small voice.

"I know buddy, I know," Alex said patting his shoulder.

"You stood, Jason." His mom said as she came over, "That's incredible"

"Yeah," Bobby said as he and Nikki came

over as well, "That was huge. You'll get there."

"There's always tomorrow," Nikki said with an understanding look, "Your leg is going to get stronger." Was it just Jason's own foul mood or was there a hint of reproach in her voice? After all Bobby wasn't going to get better tomorrow. Nikki wasn't going to wake up and find she was no longer intersex. Was it unfair of him to have hope?

Nikki said nothing bad the rest of the day and he managed to convince himself he had misread her comments. In fact Nikki, Bobby and his mom all did their best to cheer him up.

Mom had to leave by mid afternoon. She simply couldn't afford any more time off work and there were plenty of chores to do before tomorrow morning. She left with one picture of him standing triumphantly and with the news it hadn't gone any further than that.

#

The next morning Jason had a new doctor on his case. The neurologist came early and spent so long that Jason was late for physical therapy.

The neurologist poked his leg with a pin all over, making notes as he went of where the leg was numb and where, to Jason's surprise, it had no sensation at all. He brought out a small rubber hammer. Jason wondered briefly if it was wise to be hitting his leg, which was so recently broken, with any sort of hammer. The doctor did it anyway, eliciting a half dozen reflexes. Again to Jason surprise and consternation, there were times when the doctor tapped and tapped and elicited no visible response.

The neurologist was no better than any of the other doctors when it came to news. He talked gravely about how long it took for nerves to heal and indicated that swelling in the knee or further up could be pressing on the nerves, causing them to malfunction. "We will just have to wait and see," he finished. He also said something about making a brace for the ankle, which he felt to be the primary culprit in Jason's falls, not the knee. With that he was gone.

"New approach," Greg said to him when he finally made it down to physical therapy. Greg held out a pair of crutches. "We use your good leg and your two good arms to get you up and moving. Later we will get back on that," he gestured at the handlebars, "And we will see what we can do."

With the help of another therapist, Greg got Jason standing and adjusted the crutches to his height. Then he retrieved a second pair and demonstrated how to walk on them, putting all of his weight on one leg. "You can bring your right leg down to the ground and toe touch," he demonstrated as he spoke, "but don't try to put any weight on it right now."

"Cuz I'll fall on my face," Jason said ruefully.

"I don't want you falling," Greg agreed. With that they were off. He followed after Greg and found crutches far easier to master than the bars. They made three circuits of the therapy room and then practiced sitting down, getting up and even climbing stairs. By the end of the session Jason felt a lot better about his failure the day before.

"These are yours now," Greg told him, gesturing at the crutches, "and this," he kicked the chair, "its days are numbered. Understand? You can ride back to the unit but I want you up on the crutches as much as possible. As soon as your stamina starts improving, I want you coming down here on your crutches, going back to the unit on your crutches, everywhere." Jason nodded.

When Jason rolled back onto the long term ward, Alex was standing by the "nurse-server" closet writing in Jason's chart. "How was therapy today?" He asked.

"Dude," Jason replied with enthusiasm, "watch this." He pulled the brakes on the wheelchair and unloaded the crutches from his lap. He quickly set them in position and pushed himself up out of the chair.

Alex cheered as Jason started down the hall.

"Awesome, buddy!" Alex said "You're good on those things. Keep going."

Jason did, all the way down the hall. Alex strode in front of him. He stepped out into the lounge and announced, "Presenting, Jason!"

Jason came around the corner to applause. Bobby and his mother were sitting at a table playing a card game. Nikki was sitting on the couch with Alexis. Alexis was wearing her new bright yellow stocking cap, a poor replacement for the remnants of her long blond hair that they had cut off last weekend. Still she seemed in a good mood. She stood and clapped loudly as Jason made a round on his crutches. "And he's got those metal things out of his leg now." Alexis said happily. He stopped and gave her five. Nikki smiled up at him and Bobby came over and clapped him on the back. It made up in some small way, he felt, for yesterday's failing on the bars.

"This calls for a celebration," Bobby's mom said as she too came over.

"Ice Cream!" Alexis cried out hopefully.

"Oh, you don't have to go to any trouble." Jason said quickly as Bobby's mom rummaged through her purse. Jason knew Bobby's family was financially strapped by Bobby's many medical bills; like Nikki's family, like his family soon would be. He didn't want her to feel like she had to pay for everyone's treat. There must be a half dozen kids in the lounge.

Bobby must have been having the same thought because he said, "I've still got several gift vouchers in my bedside table, Mom. No point in hanging on to them."

Gift vouchers were the hospital's way of saying "we are sorry". Every department had a small stack of them. They could be used to calm an irate patient or given to family if they were stuck waiting because their loved one's test ran long. Many of the departments used them to bribe the long term pediatric cases into doing tests or what not.

The first time a radiologist had offered Jason a voucher for sitting still during an MRI he had thought it rather silly and juvenile, like getting a sucker at the doctor's office. He soon found that the vouchers were like cigarettes in jail. All the kids had a small hoard that they passed around for favors.

"Are you sure you don't want to save them?" His mother asked.

"No, I'd like to use them up," Bobby replied.

His mom gave him a sharp look. Alex came up and put one hand on her shoulder. "I'll go down with you," he said, "I can help carry. Plus my badge will get us a discount."

"Really there's no need." She replied.

"I insist," Alex said, "After all Jason is my patient."

After only a little more quibbling they left together to gather Bobby's vouchers and go to the cafeteria to get ice cream for everyone. The other kids, mostly younger kids and mostly here for chemo, quickly warmed to the idea of a party, whether or not they had any idea why they were celebrating.

Nikki, Jason and Bobby went to the table where Bobby and his mom had been playing cards.

"Wow, at this rate you'll be out of here in no time," Bobby said wistfully.

Jason was startled by the thought. Over the last six weeks this place had become his entire world. Outside this world summer was rapidly passing by, June had given way to July and August was just around the corner. All his friends were planning summer vacations, preparing for the start of fall school year and wondering where the time had gone.

Did Jason want to be out there with them, enjoy those last few days of freedom? He wasn't sure. Part of him definitely wanted to go, but part of him felt like that would be deserting his new friends. Besides what would he be doing outside of this place? It certainly wouldn't be swimming, playing touch football or planning pre-season workouts with his buddies. It wouldn't be going to keggers with Brittany.

"How soon do you think?" Nikki started to ask and then stopped.

He knew what she was asking but he had no idea what the answer was. "I don't know," he replied. He touched the bandage on his right thigh and was suddenly, illogically, comforted by it. They couldn't discharge him while he still had an open wound, could they? Granted it was much smaller than it had been; one small indent and one short expanse of beefy red. The smaller indent had healed over and most of the raw area was now a network of scar tissue. Out loud he said, "I don't think I am going home anytime soon guys. I mean I still have the wound on my leg and I need physical therapy every day."

They all nodded to each other, comforted to know their threesome wasn't going to be split up too soon. Jason caught a hint of sadness in Bobby's eyes and knew they weren't just celebrating the fact that Jason had walked (albeit on crutches) but also the fact that for today at least they were still together.

CHAPTER FOURTEEN

Bobby McGin

JASON woke in the dark. He opened his eyes and scanned around the room by the vague light coming in from the hall. He wasn't sure what had woke him. He was wide awake and knew sleep would not come again easily or quickly.

He looked over at Bobby, still trying to place what was different. It wasn't a light or a noise. It just felt too quiet.

Bobby lay on his back perfectly still. He wasn't snoring, that was what was different, Bobby wasn't snoring, he wasn't even...

Jason sat bolt upright in bed. He hurriedly pulled the covers back and found his crutches.

He didn't want to voice the end to that sentence, even in his mind, but he had to find out, just in case.

He cleared the space between the beds in two large steps. Bobby didn't even move. He lay his hand on Bobby's chest and it was perfectly still.

For a moment panic gripped Jason. What was he supposed to do? The first aid/CPR course he had taken as part of his PE class last year flashed through his mind. How many breaths per second? Or was it compressions per second?

You're in a hospital, a voice said in his head. "Of course," he thought wildly, "a hospital."

He found the red lit cross on the railing of the bed and began hitting it repeatedly. A voice crackled over the intercom, "Can I help you?" It said wearily.

"Bobby's not breathing," Jason said to the wall. "He needs help."

There was no answer but Jason heard feet pounding down the hall and a nurse appeared in the doorway.

"What happened!" She demanded.

"I don't know," Jason said, "I just woke up and he wasn't snoring or making any noise so I came over to check on him."

He was pushed aside while he was still talking. The nurse pushed her ponytail out of her way and bent over Bobby's form.

"What's going on?" Another voice called

from the doorway.

"Call a code." The first nurse said quickly.

Jason stepped back to let the nurse work. He heard a commotion in the hallway as the second nurse ran away, calling to the few other night staff that were available. The first nurse quickly dropped the bed flat and lowered the side rail. She began performing CPR. Jason wondered briefly if he should offer to help or not. One of the aides rushed and pushed him aside and began helping. Jason backed away, deciding he should let the professionals do the work.

The overhead pager system dinged distantly. Jason had taught himself to tune out the constant barrage of overhead pages but this time he heard his own room number being called.

There were more footsteps coming down the hall. A second and third nurse came barreling through the doorway. A big red pushcart, like the one his uncle used in his metal shop, was pushed through the door. The room lights came on. Under the sudden harsh glare he saw medical equipment on the top of the cart.

"Do we have IV access?" A voice asked.

"He's got a PICC," someone answered.

One of the trays slid open and an IV bag was extracted.

Jason continued to back away as more and more people filled the room. He had always thought the night shift was small, but the room was filling with more people than he had ever seen. One of the aide's kicked the brakes on Jason's bed savagely and then rolled it all the way against the wall to give the medical team more room.

Jason turned and made his way out the door. He told himself he did it to give them more room to work, not because he was terrified about what was happening.

He stepped into the hall to see a half dozen lab-coated doctors rounding the corner at something between a fast walk and a slow run. Then he understood. The overhead page was bringing staff from all over the hospital. He quickly stepped aside so they could enter the room. He heard the lead doctor shouting for information and one of the nurses responding.

A security guard rounded the corner. Wanting to avoid questions about why he was out of his room and in the hall in the middle of the night, Jason crossed the hall and went into Nikki's room.

Jason stood in the doorway for a long time, unsure what he should do. Should he wake Nikki? Should he just hide here until whatever was going on next door was finished? He didn't even want to think about what would happen when it was all finished.

"Is someone there?" He heard Nikki's voice say sleepily.

He stepped forward, framed by the light from the hall, and peered into the dark room.

He couldn't trust himself to speak.

"Jason?" She said sitting up, "Is that you? What's all the commotion out there?"

"It's Bobby." He said. "He," he didn't want to say it, "he wasn't breathing."

"Is he?" She gasped. "Oh my god!"

Having Nikki to deal with galvanized Jason somehow. He went to her bedside. She moved aside to make a space for him to sit.

"What happened?" She asked sitting up.

"I don't know," He said yet again, "I just woke up and he wasn't breathing. I called the nurse and they called," he shrugged, "everyone. They are doing everything they can."

Nikki was crying quietly at his side. "I knew," she said, "I knew the day I met him he was," She broke off and didn't say it. "I thought that meant I was prepared but I am not." She paused and asked quietly, "Do you think they'll get him back?"

He shrugged helplessly. Nikki had said exactly what he had been feeling, he knew Bobby was dying the first day. Why was this such a huge shock? But it was.

"He looked so good today," Nikki said, "He looked so happy and so good."

"He did," Jason agreed, "At the party, he was so happy."

"Do you think he knew?" She asked suddenly, "I mean he was so insistent on using up his vouchers to buy us all a treat. Did he know?"

Jason shrugged. "I don't think he could have known but I think he knew it was going to be soon. I wish I had known," He stammered, "I would have said, something."

"I loved him," Nikki admitted quietly, "I mean, you know," She looked at Jason nervously.

Jason slid his hand into hers, "I know," he said quietly. She lay her head on his shoulder. They sat that way for a long time, neither one speaking.

Jason heard a familiar voice outside in the hallway. It was Bobby's mother. Nikki heard it too and stiffened. She lifted her head as Jason rose and situated his crutches. "I'll be back," he said.

Bobby's mom was talking to one of the doctors when Jason reached the doorway. She turned at the sound of his crutches.

"What happened?" She asked him.

He shrugged, "I woke up and it was, too quiet or something. I went to his bed and he wasn't breathing. It was peaceful." He wasn't sure why he added that last bit, but it seemed like something people said about death, like it wasn't so bad someone had just died if they died peacefully.

She came to him and wrapped her arms around him. "I am sorry," She sobbed into his chest, "sorry that you had to find him like that."

Jason just stood there, unsure how to react. Her son had just died and she was worried because Jason had found him?

"Mrs. McGin?" The doctor interrupted politely from behind, "like I was saying it's been twenty five minutes and," he trailed off uncertainly.

Not turning to face the doctor she said, "You can," she choked slightly and went on. "You can stop now."

Jason heard the doctor turn back into the room. He heard the man say, "we're calling this code. Time of death 2:35 am." The sound of frenzied activity broke and a slower, softer murmur began.

Lynette McGin turned back to Jason. It was Lynette right then in Jason's mind, not Bobby's mom. Bobby's mom was too clear a reminder of Bobby. While the medical team dissembled their equipment, Lynette pulled him back into Nikki's room.

She went to Nikki's bed. "It's over," she told Nikki and held Nikki while she cried. Jason found a chair and sank heavily into it.

"There's something I want the two of you to know," Lynette said after awhile. "When," she paused and went on, "when they announced that the last chemo drug wasn't working, when we knew for sure, he," she broke off again for a time and started over, "When we knew he didn't have long left, we told him he could come home. We even had home health set up and everything."

"How soon were you planning?" Nikki asked.

"We weren't." She replied, "He refused. He didn't want to leave. He, he had friends at school, when he was younger. But after he got sick, I mean they weren't ever mean about it and a lot of those kids liked him but it was junior high and then high school and he was missing so much of the time. Their lives kept going on. He'd be in the hospital for a month here or two months there. When he got back they'd be friendly but they sort of drifted apart.

"Then this spring," she went on, "the Make a Wish Foundation came to see him. They asked what he wished for. He said the only thing he wanted was to be a normal teen with normal friends. And he knew that would never happen."

"I am sorry," Jason said.

"Don't be," she said, "because it did happen. You two gave him that. That's why even though he knew the end was coming he didn't want to leave. He didn't want to lose the two of you."

CHAPTER FIFTEEN

Turning Away

THE night and the next morning passed in a surreal daze. The nurses cleaned Bobby's body and then let Lynette, Jason and Nikki back into the room to see him one last time. Other members of Bobby's family came as well, those that lived close by.

Jason called his Aunt Mandy and she came too. She was greeted as family and in turn left with a couple of cousins in tow. They could not afford hotels locally, Mandy offered them the guest room at her house and the use of her shower before they had to return home in the morning.

Eventually however the time came for

them to move on. They were asked to step out of the room while an orderly shrouded the body. There was one last goodbye when the morgue cart rolled out of the room and down the hall. Lynette hugged him one more time and left for the front entrance to wait for her husband. Home was nearly a two hour drive away. He had not been able to make it in time. Now he would have to wait until Bobby reached the funeral home to say goodbye to his son.

With a tired hug Nikki left Jason for her room. Having nowhere else to go he returned to his room. He stared for a long time at the now empty unmade bed. He wasn't sure when he finally fell back asleep.

When he awoke he discovered that outside his little bubble of grief the rest of the hospital had continued to function as normal. Some time during the night a housekeeper and had came and made Bobby's bed. Morning had come. The day shift had arrived. Breakfast was waiting for him.

A somber Alex sat with him for awhile but he had mundane work to do. He changed Jason's dressing, an act that had become routine now for both of them. Then he asked briefly if Jason was up for Physical Therapy. Wordlessly, Jason nodded and found his crutches. In short, life went on.

After therapy he stuck his head into Nikki's room to see how she was doing. The room was empty. He panicked for a second, afraid that she too had died. But she didn't have a fatal disease, he reminded himself, and her bed was unmade, her stuff strewn everywhere.

He spotted her in the lounge. She was sitting on one of the couches, Alexis in her bright yellow hat curled up next to her. They had a book out and Nikki was reading. Her eyes were red, like she had been crying but she seemed calm. She looked up and met his gaze. She gave a weak smile.

Alexis looked up too and smiled. She waved at him. Alexis who had cancer, smiled and waved at him. Alexis who might be dying, gestured him over. He stood rooted in his spot, fighting down a sudden wave of nausea.

He shook his head and turned back towards his room. He felt terrible about doing this, running from the lounge. But he had to. He knew what he had to do. He had to keep his head down, heal and get out of here. He couldn't hang out in the lounge. He couldn't get to know these kids, or start to like them. Because they were dying.

That was unacceptable. Jason wasn't sure he could survive another Bobby-sized hole in his heart. The sorrow he felt as a physical pain, no easier to bear than the pain in his leg. There were meds for his leg at least. Nothing could stop this pain. Another hit, from Alexis, Ryan or that new boy Dylan, any of them really, could take Jason out. He couldn't risk it.

He'd talk to Nikki later. She'd understand. They weren't dying. They could hide out in his room, or hers. They could get through this together.

Jason heard Nikki's wheelchair enter his room. He wasn't sure how long he had been sitting on the edge of his bed, just sitting there. He didn't look up. He was too ashamed.

She stopped her chair beside his bed and set the brakes. She stood and sat down on the bed beside him.

"You okay?" She asked.

He nodded no, but didn't answer for a long time. Then he said, "How can you stand it, Nikki?"

"Stand what?" She asked.

"Alexis, Dylan, Kyle, any of them." He answered. "Any one of them could, they could die like..." he broke off suddenly.

"Like Bobby?" She supplied.

He nodded yes.

She shrugged and slipped her hand in his. "What am I suppose to do? Hide in my room?"

He shrugged, unwilling to say that was exactly what he was considering.

"I can't do that," she said, "they're my friends. I've got to stick by them, that's what friends do."

"What if she dies?" Jason persisted in a quiet voice.

Nikki sighed heavily and lay her head on Jason's shoulder. "I'd be so sad." She admitted, "It'd be like Bobby all over again. But you know, even though I am so tore up about Bobby, I'm glad I met him, I'm glad I got to know him."

"Me too," Jason admitted.

"Its the same with Alexis," Nikki went on, "I hope she makes it but if she doesn't, I don't want to have to think about the times I missed, the things I could have said or done with her had I known."

Jason lifted his arm and laid it over Nikki's shoulders. "You are so brave, Nikki," He told her, "and so smart."

She made a dismissive noise as she lay her head upon his shoulders again. "I wish." She said.

Bobby's mom and Aunt Mandy came in while the two of them were still sitting there. They un-entwined themselves but remained seated on the bed.

"Lynette has to get headed home, to make arrangements," Mandy told Jason and Nikki, "but she's got to get his stuff and she wanted to say her goodbyes."

They nodded. Nikki stood and gave Lynette a hug. "I am going to miss you," Nikki told her, "and him." She nodded at the empty bed and started crying again.

"I know, we all will." Lynette told her. Jason stood too and accepted a hug from Lynette.

"I don't know what I am going to do with most of this stuff, but I can't just leave it." She said looking over at Bobby's side of the room. "If there's anything either of you two want, please. It's the least I can do. You want the

Xbox?" She said to Jason, "I know you two played a lot."

Jason looked at the white box that he was being offered. It felt like too much. His friendship with Bobby had been real. It had saved him in those days right after his accident, when everything else had been so crazy. To be rewarded for it, like he hadn't done it for Bobby's sake, seemed dishonest somehow. Especially with something as big as an Xbox.

"I can't," He said, "besides I have one at home." The unit had one too in the lounge but most of the games he and Bobby had gathered were too mature for the other patients.

"Are you sure?" Lynette persisted, "It won't get used at our place."

He found his crutches and crossed to the machine. He pulled the memory card out and held it up. "His avatar," he said. Aunt Mandy and Lynette gave him blank looks but Nikki nodded knowingly. The memory card contained not only Bobby's profile but a profile and online Avatar they had created together called "cancer boy" based on the inside joke they shared with Dan.

Taking the memory card he went to the bedside table. He opened the top drawer and removed a dark blue stocking cap, one of about six that were in the drawer. Bobby had worn them constantly. He held one out to Nikki.

"Yes, please." She replied holding her

hand out. She took the cap and held it to her cheek.

He took one too and went back to the bed. "Are you sure about the Xbox?" Aunt Mandy asked one last time.

"I don't think I'll be playing for awhile." Jason said. "And mom can bring mine if I change my mind."

Lynette gathered up Bobby's possessions. An aide came in and assisted her in putting the stuff on a cart. With one more hug she was gone. Aunt Mandy promised she'd be right back and they'd all do something for supper, but she wanted to walk Lynette out.

The next morning while Jason was waiting for rehab, he heard raised voices in the hallway outside his room. Despite his mood, curiosity got the better of him and he got up on his crutches to peer out his door.

A middle aged heavy set woman was standing at the nurse server across the hall, Nikki's nurse server. She had short red hair. She wore a long gray skirt, a silky gray blouse and dangling hoop earrings. On top of her blouse was a white lab coat that marked her as a doctor. The seemingly omnipresent stethoscope was missing but the breast pocket was overloaded with pens, tools and a thick name badge.

On the other side of the nurse server was a tall thin grayed haired man in a tweed suit. It was someone Jason recognized instantly, Nikki's psychiatrist. He struck his open left hand on the top of the nurse server's fold down table to the rhythm of his words."I can not believe you told my patient this nonsense," He said.

"She's my patient too." The woman responded sharply, "And she asked for her test results."

"He," The psychiatrist answered with a strong emphasis, "is still a child. And your little stunt in there is threatening years of work by myself and that boy's parents."

"Nikki is fifteen," the woman replied, "a minor, yes, but a child, no! She has the right to question her care."

Jason ducked into the restroom of his room, where he could hear the conversation without being seen. He smiled at the woman's defense of Nikki and wondered if this was the Beth he'd heard about.

"I have been Nick's primary psychiatrist for nearly fourteen years now," the man was saying. "We have ran tests and he is a boy."

"You ran tests fourteen years ago," The woman shot back, slapping the table for emphasis. "DNA tests. We have come a long way in our understanding of gender identity in fourteen years, Dr. Kinnick. I've done MRI studies of Nikki's brain, I've looked at her hormone profiles and I've interviewed her extensively. We've done personality tests, you name it. It's time to face the truth, whatever you found fourteen years ago what I'm seeing right now is a fairly normal fifteen year old girl." She emphasized the girl at the end of the sentence.

"And that's what you told him?" Dr. Kinnick shot back.

"Yes, she asked and I told her!" The woman responded.

"In defiance of the established protocol set by the entire treatment team?" He demanded.

"I don't answer to you," the woman said, "I don't answer to Dr. Hausbender," Dr. Hausbender, Jason knew, was Nikki's surgeon. "I don't even answer to Nikki's parents," she went on, "I answer to Nikki. She's my patient."

"Still," he said, "You don't determine the plan of care. That was set in a care conference earlier this summer. Do you understand?"

"Then maybe we need to have another care conference." The woman insisted. There was the sound of retreating feet as one of them stormed off. He looked out the door and saw Dr. Kinnick still standing in the hallway scowling. He noticed Jason and his scowl deepened.

Jason looked down quickly and made his way out in the hallway, heading towards therapy. When he had passed the psychiatrist he lifted his head and smiled. Nikki, it seemed, had at least one doctor who understood her.

CHAPTER SIXTEEN

Letting Go

NIKKI was waiting in the hallway when Jason got back from the physical therapy. He wanted to talk to her about what he'd overheard but she nodded down the hall and said, "you ready?"

"Is it time already?" He asked.

She nodded, "Almost."

He sighed. He looked towards his room. "Yeah, just let me," Then he stopped and shrugged. There was nothing in his room he needed. "I guess I am ready."

They went together towards the lounge. The tables had been moved to one side. The couch had been repositioned and every chair had been stolen from every conference room on the floor. A large picture of Bobby had been stood on an easel at the front of the chairs. A couple of vases of plastic flowers stood on a desk nearby. Real flowers were not allowed on the unit. Some of the kids were so sick, their immune systems so weak, that even trace amounts of pollen could make them sick.

Almost all of them were too sick to go to Bobby's funeral. A "pass" to leave the hospital was a rare thing. Nikki was well enough to go, but her parent's couldn't get the day off. She said she didn't want to go anyway. How could she sit in a church full of strangers and mourn Bobby? Jason had asked about it, even though he kind of agreed with Nikki. His orthopedic surgeon had been in favor of it but the infectious disease doctor that was taking care of the wound in his leg was unsure. Jason had let the issue drop. He couldn't see making his mom miss yet another day of work either.

For the rest of the kids there was no way they could leave and make the three hour drive to Bobby's hometown. So the funeral came to them. The hospital pastoral care department would officiate. The nurses and other patients would be given a chance to speak if they wished to.

He found a seat on the aisle, so that Nikki could park her wheelchair next to him. When he saw Alexis coming down the hall he slid down a seat and patted the chair he had just vacated. He figured it was what Nikki wanted.

Alexis took the chair next to him and then snuggled against Jason's side. He put his arms around her. He knew suddenly Nikki was right. Holding Alexis at a distance because of what happened to Bobby would only make it worse if she too died. He kissed her forehead and told her it would be okay. He glanced up to find Nikki smiling at him through eyes wet with tears. Their hands found each other.

The pastor coughed for everyone's attention and the service started. Later Jason would remember almost nothing of what was actually said at the service. He would remember the feel of Alexis snuggled against his side, and of Nikki's hand in his.

#

Over the next few days a new routine set in for Jason and Nikki. Jason would often find Nikki in the lounge when he got back from therapy. That's where they would spend most of their morning. For Jason Black Ops and Halo with Bobby gave way to Lego Star Wars and Mario Cart with eight year old Ryan. Nikki would read to Alexis, or the two would play a game together.

After lunch Nikki and Jason would wander the hospital. There was only so much of the lounge they could take, all the other kids were so much younger. By unspoken agreement they avoided the places where the three of them had hung out together. Instead they found new places. It wasn't hard. The hospital was riddled with lounges, waiting areas and conference rooms. The cafeteria had a deck and when the sun wasn't too hot it was nice to sit outside and pretend they weren't hospitalized at all.

They discovered that one of the outpatient clinics had moved recently. There was a waiting room just below the balcony that the three of them had frequented that currently was not connected to any office. Jason would take his iPad and the two of them would watch funny youtube clips or surf the net in peace, cuddled together on a small loveseat out of sight.

Without Bobby there to distract him in the evenings, Jason developed a morbid habit of re-watching his old football games on the iPad. It wasn't healthy, he didn't think, but he couldn't stop himself.

#

Four days after Bobby's memorial service he managed to talk both Alexis and Nikki into joining him and Ryan on Mario Cart. Before long he had both the girls laughing.

Out of the corner of his eye he saw a form enter the lounge, the woman's messy reddish-brown hair matched Nikki's and the thin hunched form bore a family resemblance as well. Her face was different, not the pinched features that Nikki or her father had. Her cheeks were wider, more jowly. Still there could be little doubt who this was. Jason hit pause as Nikki caught sight of her mother.

"Don't stop on my account," Mrs. Pagan

said, "I can wait until your game is done."

"It's just a game," Nikki said dismissively, setting down the controller. Alexis too surrendered her controller with barely a shrug. Ryan squawked, "C'mon, just finish this race!"

Jason gave him a sympathetic look. He felt like they could have easily finished out this race before quitting but apparently the girls didn't care.

"You want to go someplace, mom?" Nikki asked.

"Not just yet," Mrs. Pagan replied, "Your primary nurse is on break." Nikki made a face. Her primary nurse was Andrea, also known as McBitch. "I've got to talk to her before we can go anywhere. They want to schedule another one of those care conference things."

Nikki gave her mom a grim look. "Yeah, they do," She agreed.

"You know?" Her mom asked.

"I heard them talking about it," Nikki replied evasively. Jason thought back to the argument that Beth and Dr. Kinnick had had. It was loud enough he was sure Nikki had heard it as well. There was going to be a showdown between the Nikki's psychiatrist and her Endocrinologist about her gender. But would it come too late for Nikki?

Her mom shrugged. "It makes sense," she said, "to do it now before you come home."

There was a pause and then Nikki said, "Who all is going to be there?"

"I don't know, most of the doctor's I think." Her mother replied.

"I mean, is dad coming too?" Nikki clarified.

"If he can get the time off." Her mother said.

"Beth, Dr. Wilson," Nikki said, "thinks it would be best if you are both there to hear what she has to say."

Her mother shrugged helplessly, "I will see what I can do."

Jason arrived back from Physical Therapy the next morning to find Nikki in his room, along with Alexis, Ryan and even Alex and another nurse.

"It was her idea," Alex said with a gesture towards Nikki, "but it's a good idea."

He looked towards Nikki. She had made a cross out of construction paper and string and was wearing it around her neck. On his bedside table she had set up his iPad. It was displaying a picture of him in uniform, probably from one of the articles in the local paper about him. On either side were two of the plastic flowers they had used for Bobby's memorial.

"Have a seat," Nikki said, gesturing towards his bed. "I noticed the other day that all your most viewed videos are of old games." He shrugged but didn't deny it.

Alex came over and sat beside him. He put his arm around Jason's shoulders. "You are a great kid, Jason. There are a million things you can do with your life." He said.

"I'll never play ball again," Jason said quietly.

"No, you won't," Alex agreed sadly.

"You need to move on," Nikki said placing a hand on his knee, "Alex is right, there are a million things you can do. But first you have to accept this one thing that you can't."

"So?" He said with a nod towards the iPad.

"So we are going to hold a memorial," Nikki said, "for Jason the ball player. So you can start to put him to rest, and become Jason the kid again."

Nikki played the part of the priest. It was goofy but as she talked Jason found his eyes tearing up. At Nikki's prompting he stood and gave himself a short eulogy.

"Jason was a hard worker and good player," he said, "He just wanted people to like him, he wanted to be part of something." He paused as images of that last night rushed upon him, the drinking, Brittany, the argument about driving. He sat down heavily on the bed. "Sometimes he tried too hard to fit in," he finished lamely.

Nikki, he knew, understood what he had just said. Alex apparently had too. "Jason was a great ballplayer and a great athlete," he said. He patted Jason on the shoulder, "but this Jason is a much better man."

The afternoon of his memorial was quiet. He and Nikki watched a few videos but spoke little. After she headed back to her room, he ate his supper and read until the evening nurse came to do the nightly dressing change. It was a book Nikki had gotten him started reading. He didn't think he would ever be the avid reader that Nikki was, but he was learning that he did enjoy some books. More importantly, for the first time in weeks he wasn't watching his old games. They were right, it was time to let that part of his life go.

CHAPTER SEVENTEEN

A Knight in Shiny Lab Coat

THE next day after his morning rehab session Jason went to find Nikki to thank her for the memorial idea. She wasn't in the lounge.

Turning back towards her room he saw a man leaving. The man was slender and appeared to be somewhere in his thirties at the oldest. He was dressed in slacks and a white shirt. A blazer was hung casually over the loops on the messenger bag he had at his side. He stopped briefly to look back in the room and wave at Nikki before he headed down the hall.

Jason made for Nikki's room. Did doctor's

have to wear white lab coats? How much of the stuff they carried was actually necessary for their jobs and how much was just to identify them as doctors? Beth had been the only doctor he had seen so far that didn't carry a stethoscope. After Nikki explained exactly what an endocrinologist was and did, it made sense. But then again Dr. Kinnick did carry a stethoscope. Why would a psychiatrist need to listen to your heart?

Still, why would a grown man who was obviously a professional, be visiting Nikki if he was not a doctor? The man must have been a doctor.

Nikki was looking at the cover of a book when he entered the room. Her eyes were misty and vacant and she was turning the book over in her hands rather than reading it.

"Hey," he said from the doorway.

"Hey Jason, come in," she said.

"Who was that?" He asked nodding towards the hallway. "Another Doctor?"

"Hmm," she hummed and nodded yes.

"Good doctor?" He guessed by her mood.

"Best yet," she said, "I think I'll dub him my knight in shiny lab coat."

Jason sank into a chair by the bed, where Nikki was sitting. "Wow, that's quite an honor." He said.

Nikki shook her head and came to herself slightly, "Yeah, but he deserves it. That was Doctor Daniel Diamond." She said.

"What's he a doctor of?" Jason asked.

"Actually he's not a medical doctor," she replied, "He's a geneticist."

"Really?" Jason joked, "Branching out now are we?"

She smiled at him and threw her pillow at his face. He caught it easily.

"Beth sent a blood sample to the University of Montana, where he works." Nikki said, "They ran a huge DNA profile for her. Daniel was in town for a conference at the University here and decided to stop by and see me personally." She ended with a smug look and stuck her tongue out at him.

"Well, he sure put you in a good mood," Jason said. "What did he have to say."

"I'm loopy." She said with a laugh.

"I could have told them all that without a genetic profile." He replied.

She laughed again, "I might be transgender after all." She said.

"Huh?"

"He said they've been working on genetic research with people who identify as transgender and some of them have anomalies in their DNA. Being transgender might end up being a medical condition after all, a genetic one at that. What they found in my DNA is similar to that condition, only I have it worse."

"What condition is that?" Jason asked.

"My testosterone receptor sites are loopy." She said.

"Okay, now you've completely lost me." He said.

"The receptor sites," she began and then catching his blank look, "The places where testosterone attaches to the cell, they aren't shaped right so it can't do what it's supposed to."

"Okay, so that's great?" He ventured.

She snatched the pillow from him and hit him with it playfully. "Yes it is, dork!" She laughed, "You know why?"

He shook his head no, holding his hands out to ward off the pillow. "No," he said, "I've only had basic science for dummies."

"It means," she explained, "That all those shots I have been getting to make me a boy, the testosterone shots, they don't work on me anyway. They might as well have been shooting me with water."

She sighed and sat the pillow down, suddenly serious again. "I'll never really be a girl either. I don't have a womb. I can't be a mother. But I'll also never be a boy. I'll just be me, for the rest of my life. Nikki."

"You don't have to be anything different, Nikki," Jason said, "because you are great just like you are."

She smiled at him and slid closer, "thanks," she said and kissed him on the cheek. Jason blushed.

He caught her hand as she slid back away from him. "Seriously," he said, "you are a great person." Their eyes met and they stared at each other for a long moment.

She broke the gaze first, scooping the

book up from the bed. "He left me this book," She said. She held it up for him to see. It was called Evolution's Rainbow. "Its written by a geneticist but its for normal people. He says its a great introduction to what modern genetics has to say about sexuality and gender and all that. He thinks it might help me understand my condition better, learn how to cope and stuff."

"Cool," He replied.

"Yeah, but you know what?" She added suddenly, "None of that is really why he's my knight in shiny lab coat. It was something else."

"What was that?" Jason asked.

"I asked him, at the end of our little talk, what he thought. Am I a boy or a girl?" She looked at Jason and smiled, "You know what he said?"

Jason shook his head no.

"He just shrugged and said, it doesn't matter. Be whatever you want."

#

Jason looked up from the book he was reading to Alexis and sighed. Nikki gave him a short irritated look and then looked back down at her book.

He knew the irritated look wasn't for him, but it stung nonetheless. He wished Nikki could be curled up on the couch with him and Alexis but that wasn't possible today for several reasons.

The first of these was the IV pole that

Alexis currently sported. It was her treatment day. As with Bobby, the treatment would have almost no apparent effect while it was running, it would be tonight and tomorrow that she would suffer. Jason however suffered right away. The IV pole and the term "treatment day" were painful reminders of why these kids were here, and what could very easily happen to them.

The other reason Nikki couldn't, or wouldn't, sit next to him was her mother's presence. They were sharing the second couch that lay perpendicular to where Jason and Alexis were reading. It was better than having Nikki's dad around but not by much. Her mom acceded to her child's wish to be called "Nikki" but then screwed up at least half the time and used Nick anyway. Then there was the somewhat constant barrage of mis-gendering. It was drawing irritated looks from Nikki and confused ones from Alexis.

"Why does she keep calling Nikki he?" Alexis had whispered when Nikki's mom pushed her back to her room to use the restroom.

"It's complicated," Jason told her. She accepted this explanation with a shrug.

Then there was the book, Evolution's Rainbow. Nikki was trying to explain it to her mother. It was a roundabout way of discussing Nikki's own situation. Her mother seemed to sense that as well. She would nod politely when Nikki read her a piece or explained something. But whenever Nikki tried to start a discussion, her mother would merely say something like, "You've got really good doctors here, hun" or "we are just trying to do what's best for you."

"You don't know what's best for me!" Nikki finally snapped back at her mother.

"Your doctors...." her mom started.

"They don't know what's best for me either!" Nikki interrupted.

"And I suppose you do?" Her mom snapped back.

Nikki fell silent.

"You're fifteen." Her mother reminded her.

"I know what's not best." Nikki muttered darkly, looking away.

The real reason for Nikki's mood was the same reason that her mother was here in the first place. Tomorrow was Nikki's second procedure. Tomorrow the loop of flesh they had built between her legs would be cut and shaped into a penis. Tomorrow Nikki was to become a boy.

Jason sighed and returned his attention to the book. He felt terrible for Nikki. Worst of all, he felt powerless. It was worse, in ways, then Bobby's death. Bobby's death had been tragic but unavoidable. He could rage against fate or god. What was happening to Nikki was neither unavoidable or an act of fate. It was an act of people, an injustice being carried out by people who thought they were acting in her "best interest".

#

The next morning Jason stood in the doorway of his room, impatient. His leg was sore from standing so long in one place, but he wasn't about to budge either. There was something he was bound and determined not to miss.

Nikki's mom had spent the night in one of the hospitals "hostel" rooms a cheap alternative to a hotel. She would stay both today and tomorrow. Her father had arrived yesterday evening and would stay through the evening tonight.

Jason had set the alarm on his iPad to wake him early this day, but he was so keyed up that he had woken as soon as he heard the day shift start to arrive at 6:30 in the morning. On his way to the bathroom he had seen Nikki's parents arrive and go into the room.

He had purposefully taken a long time about his morning toiletries, peering out of the bathroom door occasionally to watch nurses come and go from Nikki's room. They had rolled the transport gurney into the room almost ten minutes ago and Jason had discarded any pretense of doing anything other than waiting.

Finally the door opened and the cart rolled out into the hall. They parked it perpendicular to the respective doorways while the transporter got Nikki's chart out of the nurse server.

He took a step forward and his knee

buckled, nearly dropping him to the floor. "Smooth move ex-lax," he said to himself. The next step held him up and he got out into the hallway without embarrassing himself further.

Andrea, Nikki's primary nurse, was there and shot him a dark disapproving look. He ignored it and went to Nikki's side.

She was dressed in a hospital gown, with a sheet over her. An IV was attached to one arm and the bag hung from a stand on the cart itself.

She looked up at him. She looked small, pale and frightened. It looked as though she had been crying. Their eyes met and she mouthed, "I don't want this."

He mouthed back, "I know." Out loud he said, "Just come back safe, okay?"

She nodded. Her parents came out of the room and he greeted them with a nod. With that they were gone, Nikki being rolled down the hall and off the unit.

He turned back into his room. He climbed back in bed and waited passively for his day nurse to come with breakfast, then to do his dressing change, and then for therapy. After that he had no idea. Perhaps he would wait in the lounge, or in his room. It would be noon or later before Nikki would be out of surgery. It might even be evening, depending on how long they kept her in recovery.

#

News came in shortly before lunchtime. Jason was in the lounge playing Lego Star

Wars on the Wii with Ryan and being beaten terribly. This was in large part because Jason kept jumping every time he heard a noise, looking down the hall to see if it was Nikki.

A hand on his shoulder made him jump again. It was Angie, his nurse for the day. She leaned in close and whispered in his ear, "Quit being so jumpy. Nikki's fine. She won't be back until late this afternoon and you probably won't get to see her until tomorrow, but she's out of surgery and it went perfectly according to plan. She's awake and doing good."

She turned and started to walk away. Relief flooded Jason, followed by gratitude. They weren't supposed to talk about other patients, he knew that. "Hey, Angie?" He called after her. She stopped and turned back. "Thanks," he said.

She smiled and winked at him.

CHAPTER EIGHTEEN

A Knight on Shiny Crutches

JASON woke to the sound of crying. He closed his eyes in the dark and listened to it. He remembered his first few days in the hospital and the sound of Nikki crying herself to sleep. There was something different about this.

For starters she hadn't done this in a long while. She'd cried plenty. The girl was a prodigious waterworks. During the first few days after Bobby's death Jason had worried she'd dehydrate from the big wet tears that fell almost constantly. She cried when she was mad, she cried when she was sad, sometimes she even cried when she was happy. But it had been a long time since she had cried alone. After Bobby's death she had cried big wet patches on his shoulder during the day, but at night it was quiet.

That was part of it, but the sounds of her tears were different too. He tried to put a name or description to how they were different. They were huge racking sobs, he decided. He couldn't understand why the night staff hadn't heard them and gone to check on her.

He slid the covers off and found a pair of the hospital's no skid booty socks for his feet. He pulled a T shirt over his head. Dressed in that and his baggy sweats, he hoisted himself up on his crutches and padded across his room.

He paused and peered both ways down the hallway. The nurses station was about halfway down and brightly lit. He heard a chair creak but otherwise it was silent. He saw the form of one of the aides leave one room and disappear into another. Cautiously, he slid out into the hall and across to Nikki's room.

"Hey Nikki," he said quietly from the doorway. "Are you okay?"

The sobs stopped. "No," her voice came back softly.

He entered her room and went to her bedside. A pale night light shown on her face, which looked even more pale, frightened and sunken then it had in the morning.

"They said it went well this morning." He

said.

She nodded. "I felt fine after. Now," she stopped and stared off into space, "I feel like there's this black maw that's devouring me, I am sinking."

"Does it hurt?" He asked.

She nodded no. "I can't put a finger on it. I just feel numb. I am scared, Jason. I think something is wrong, down there." She nodded towards her crotch.

"Did you," he paused awkwardly, not really wanting to say it, "Did you check?"

"I can't," she said quietly, "I just can't. I am so scared but I can't bring myself to look."

Jason swallowed hard. He had never seen her so scared before. It scared him. Was she dying?

She was his friend. More than that, he loved her. He had to admit it now. And that meant he had to do something for her, something he really didn't want to do. He'd have to look.

He paused. Could he handle it? There are things that can't be unseen. What if he looked and she was, a boy. What if he saw the work they did and it changed how he viewed Nikki? Would it change how he felt?

Worse still what if it didn't change how he felt? Jason didn't have anything against gay people, but he didn't think he was gay. But what if he saw Nikki down there, saw a boy and still had feelings for her? Could he even wrap his head around that?

A sob quietly hiccuped it's way out of Nikki, bringing him back to the present. He had no choice. He owed Nikki big time.

"It's going to be okay," He said and slowly lifted the sheets. "Oh god!" He said and dropped the sheets again. He looked away. Not daring to look back he found himself once again frantically hitting the nurse's call light.

Nikki's hand found his and he held it tight. A bored voice came over the intercom. "What do you need, Nikki?"

"Someone needs to come down here right away." Jason answered.

At least, he told himself, it did not look like a penis. Nor did it look like a part of Nikki at all. It looked, if anything, like a bloated, swollen bratwurst had been dropped on her lap; a bratwurst that was slowly turning purple.

Footsteps came down the hallway. The night nurse gave him a sharp look. "I heard her crying and came to see what was wrong. She thought something was wrong down there so I looked." He said quickly, fighting down a wave of nausea. "There is," he finished.

The nurse lifted the sheets and made a face.

"Do we need to call a code?" A male aide asked from the doorway, concern in his voice.

"No," the nurse replied decisively, "but I do want a set of vitals right away."

The aide disappeared. The nurse ignored Jason and began to do something with the IV machine. It started to whine as the speed of the drip was increased.

"Can I help?" Another nurse said as she entered the room.

"Call the supervisor," the first nurse told her, "Tell her we need the surgical team called in." The second nurse turned and left.

The aide came back with a blood pressure machine and began strapping it to Nikki's arm. The nurse went out in the hallway, pulling a cellphone out as she did so. They could hear easily from the room as she talked on it.

"Yes, I need to speak to Dr. Hausbender right away." She said and then, "I don't care who the on-call doctor is, I need Dr. Hausbender." There was a pause and then, "No! You don't understand, this is a special case of Dr. Hausbender's. I need to talk to him, not the on-call." Then finally a not very sincere, "Thank you."

With the doctor her tone was quieter and more respectful. Jason couldn't catch everything, but he caught more than enough. "Graft failure" "nearly complete" "no, it can't wait" "blood poisoning" and finally, "the surgical team is already being called in."

An older nurse came in. She had gray hair, a scowling face and a walk that spoke of authority. "Better not be a false alarm." She muttered darkly, "I've gotten the entire surgical team woken and on their way." Without introducing herself to Nikki or Jason she lifted the sheets. Her expression changed immediately. "Not a false alarm." She said. The nurse, who had returned to room, gave her an exasperated look.

Two residents wandered in. Even without an overhead page, apparently news of Nikki's complication was spreading. They too lifted the sheets without bothering to introduce themselves. After inspecting it closely they walked out into the hallway, pulling tablet computers out of their pockets as they went.

The next doctor was a female and she did introduce herself. "Hello, I am Dr. Chang," she said shaking Nikki's hand. "I am the senior surgical resident. I am going to take a quick look and then I'll talk to you, okay?"

Nikki nodded as yet another person lifted the sheets. Dr. Chang nodded thoughtfully before turning her attention back to Nikki.

"Do you know what's going on?" She asked Nikki.

Eyes still wide, Nikki nodded no.

"Well it looks like the graft is failing, it's not getting enough blood circulation." Dr. Chang said. "But the real problem right now is this, the blood that is getting to the graft isn't moving fast enough and it's dying. If those dead blood cells get back into circulation that can cause some pretty serious complications for you. What we need to do is to get you back down to surgery right away. Your doctor is on his way and will meet us down there. Hopefully, we can save the graft, but the most important thing right now is protecting you.

That might mean removing some or even all of the graft tissue." Nikki nodded.

"Is she going to be okay?" Jason demanded. Dr. Chang look around the room, momentarily confused by who Jason was or why he was there.

"Yes," she responded after a moment's hesitation. "We have caught it in time, barely, but in time. We'll probably have to give him some antibiotics, but his life isn't in danger. Now if this had gone until morning?" She shrugged.

A cart was being pushed in the doorway. Jason backed up and sat in one of the chairs to be out of the way while they loaded Nikki onto the cart and took off with her.

They left abruptly, apparently forgetting about Jason's presence altogether. He stayed in the chair. There was no way he could go back to sleep now even if he wanted to. Besides he wasn't leaving this room, no matter what anyone said, until he knew for sure that Nikki was okay. He braced himself mentally for the argument with the night nurse but apparently the events surrounding Nikki completely obliterated any thought of Jason being out of his room well past midnight.

He sat in the semi-darkened room by himself for what seemed like an eternity. He didn't move, he barely so much as thought, aside from praying that Nikki would be okay.

His reverie was interrupted by a soft gasp as Nikki's mom walked into the room and saw him.

"What?" She began looking towards the door in confusion.

"He was the one who found your son crying," The nurse said as she entered behind the woman, "And called for help. Though, I would have thought he'd have gone back to his own room by now." She ended with a sharp look.

"I just want to know she's - Nikki's going to be okay," he said. He met the nurse's gaze defiantly.

"It's okay," Nikki's mom said, defusing some of the tension, "He and the other boy, the one who passed away, they've been good friends for Nick this summer. I don't mind if he stays."

The nurse nodded and promised to let them know the second she heard anything. With that she was gone. Nikki's mom perched on Nikki's bed, clutching her purse.

"Nick was crying?" She said after some time.

"Yeah," he replied. He paused. He really wanted to call her Nikki and she, to show his support but her mother saw Nikki as a he, her son. Finally he just went on, "Nikki said something felt wrong, it wasn't pain exactly, just a sinking feeling, like the life was draining out." It felt awkward and stilted to talk without using pronouns. "I called for the nurse."

"Thank you," she said quietly. She started rocking slightly. She dug into her purse and came out with a wadded tissue. She used it to dab at her eyes. "I just want what's best for my child." She said suddenly, "That's all me and Larry ever wanted for Nick, what's best." She looked at Jason intently while she said it, as though daring him to deny it.

Helpless in the face of her sorrow he just shrugged. "I know," He said, "And I know the doctor's know a lot of stuff, but even they don't know everything. I mean look at that geneticist that came last week, he's like the best in the nation or something. Even he wasn't completely sure."

She nodded slightly, "I just hope he's okay."

Jason reached across and took her hand. "Me too." He said consolingly. They sat in silence for a long time.

#

The light flicked on as a man entered. He was tall and broad. He had wavy dark hair. He had a long narrow nose and chiseled cheekbones. He was dressed in surgical scrubs. Even before he opened his mouth to speak, Jason could sense his arrogance.

"Aah, Mrs. Pagan," he said as he approached the bed, "I am so sorry to see you again in this way."

Jason was half out of his seat, as was Nikki's mom. The man, who Jason guessed had to be Dr. Hausbenber, the plastic surgeon he heard so much about, waved them back. "Never fear," he chided, "Nicholas is quite safe and whole. He made it through the surgery quite beautifully, really. His vitals are stable and he'll be back to the floor in just a few minutes."

Dr. Hausbender half sat, half leaned against the bed, "Now, as far as the graft, we were not so lucky. If you will remember what we discussed last spring, how we must give it time to create a new blood supply?" He said to Nikki's mom. Dr. Chang, the surgical intern, came into the room and leaned against the wall. She gave Jason a short nod of recognition. "We talked about how one possible complication was that it would not create enough of a blood supply to support the new appendage. Remember that?"

She nodded.

"It's rare, very rare." He said.

Dr. Chang's eyebrow went up slightly and Jason wondered suddenly if Dr. Hausbender was telling the truth.

"Well, everything had indicated that Nicholas's body had formed a sufficient blood supply to the pedicle but alas it wasn't. Much of it was already necrotic and we had no choice but to remove the entire thing." Dr. Hausbender went on.

"It failed?" Nikki's mom asked quietly.

"No, no, no" Dr. Hausbender said taking her hand and patting it in what Jason thought was an extremely patronizing way. "Not failure, merely a setback. Complications happen. We manage them." He shrugged as if to say no big deal. "Now we took the skin graft from Nicholas's right thigh," He pointed to the area on his own thigh, "We can try again, using the left thigh. If we absolutely have to we take skin from elsewhere but that's not as good."

Jason stared at the doctor, the words 'try again' ringing in his ears. They couldn't possibly be serious? He looked at Nikki's mom. She was looking at the doctor with a look of absolute trust. He looked at Dr. Chang, she at least looked a little suspicious at the doctor's rosy prognosis.

"But school starts in another three weeks," Nikki's mom said quietly, "will that be enough time?"

"No, no," Dr. Hausbender laughed, "We must first give his body some time to heal. It will take a long time again, but there's no rush. Maybe next summer." He patted her on the knee. "For now the residents will handle the day to day, I will check in on Nicholas's progress from time to time and we will plan a consultation again later in the year. Alright?"

She nodded and he was gone.

Jason's mind burned. 'Try again' was now competing with 'next summer' in his mind. He felt a white hot anger inside him. They couldn't do this. They couldn't put Nikki through another summer of laying in a hospital bed, crying herself to sleep every night trying to make her into something she's not. He wouldn't stand for it. Helplessness fueled his rage further. What could he do?

"Mrs. Pagan?" Dr. Chang said softly after Dr. Hausbender was gone. "It's going to be okay now. We got the graft off before there was any real sign of blood poisoning. We are going to keep Nick-ee" She stumbled over the name, unsure which was correct, "on some antibiotics for a time but things should heal pretty well on their own now."

There was a rattling in the hallway and a cart rolling up to the room.

"And the surgery?" Nikki's mom was saying, "what he said about trying again?"

"That's not really her call." a voice said from the doorway. It was Andrea, aka McBitch. She still had her purse under her arm, as though she had just walked on the unit, which given the time of day was likely. Behind her a cart rolled in the room with Nikki on it. She looked pale, but more peaceful. Andrea went on, "nor is it really Dr. Hausbender's call. But we will discuss that in the care conference. For now we just have to get this one better." She pointed a finger at Nikki, who was watching her sleepily. "No more scares out of you," Andrea said to her. Nikki gave a wan smile and nod.

"And you best be getting back to your own room." She threw at Jason. Guiltily, he stood and mouthed a "welcome home" to Nikki before he left.

#

It was late afternoon before Jason got to see or talk to Nikki again. He ate his breakfast, had his morning dressing change and went to physical therapy. On his way back to the room he saw that Nikki had company. Both of her parents and several other people, family members probably, were there. He did not want to disturb them.

He told himself he would check back later but when he got back to his room he crashed hard. He had been awake the better part of the night. He slept until almost one in the afternoon and had to have them reheat his lunch for him.

After he had eaten he passed her room again but her company was still there. He went to the lounge and found Alexis looking a bit lost without either of them around. He told her that Nikki had had some problems during the night but was okay now. He wasn't sure when she'd be out in the lounge again.

Finally on his way back to his room after spending most of the afternoon playing Wii with Ryan and Alexis, he saw the visitors leaving Nikki's room. He told the kids he had to go and went to her door.

She was laying with her head faced away from him. At first he thought she was sleeping, but she turned when she heard his crutches.

"Hey," she called and he went to her bedside. She was still pale and looked weak but her color was better and she smiled up at him.

She pulled one hand free of the blankets and he took it in his.

"You're going to be okay now?" He asked.

She nodded yes. "I've got a new knight too." She said.

"Oh really?" He asked.

She ran her knuckles along the edge of his crutches, "Yeah," She said, "A knight on shiny crutches."

Jason blushed heavily. "Goofball," he told her.

"You saved my life." She insisted.

"It was nothing." He replied. "So now what?"

She shrugged tiredly, "Back to square one, I guess."

They held each other's gaze for a few minutes then Nikki sighed, "Let's talk about something else."

He nodded. He pulled a chair over and sat.

CHAPTER NINETEEN

A Looming Discharge

THAT night Jason tossed and turned. The subdued night time noises of the hospital no longer bothered him, but he still couldn't sleep. He kept thinking of Nikki.

She was out of the woods, they had assured him. She was feeling weak but already better. Her color had improved just from last night. It was hard to shake the image of her in the dim light, so pale and scared.

That wasn't what was keeping him awake though. It was Dr. Hausbender, tall, handsome and arrogant. The glib "try again" rolled around and around in Jason's brain. It made him seethe with anger. It was bad enough that he had done this too Nikki, that he wanted to do it all over again was unthinkable.

Or at least it was unthinkable to Jason. He was worried it wasn't so unthinkable for anyone else. Nikki's mom had seemed so uncertain, so close to accepting that the doctor's didn't know what they were doing, when it was just her and Jason. But once the doctor showed up she just seemed to go blank. Jason had known when he saw that look that she didn't have it in her to question the doctor's authority. That challenge was up to someone else.

It wasn't going to be Nikki either. She would rage at him, like she had raged at Bobby. Then she snipped at her mom. But she was too beaten down by years of dealing with these issues. She would make a feeble protest to one of her doctors and when they didn't listen, she'd clam up. All they ever saw was a typical surly teenager. They didn't see how their decisions really affected her. They were not here when she cried herself to sleep at night. Most of all, they could not see the warm vivacious girl she could be if they would just let her.

Beth did see it and Jason was glad she was involved in Nikki's case. He hoped she could sway the other doctors but he had his fears too. The hospital was one huge bureaucracy. He had observed that more times than he cared to admit. Beth didn't seem like the kind of woman that would back down from a fight, but she wasn't Nikki's primary doctor either. If she said one thing but Dr. Hausbender or Dr. Kinnick said another, who would win? Probably not Beth.

There wasn't much Jason could do, except be there for Nikki. And he wasn't sure how much longer he could do that. He was up on his crutches almost all day now. He was rapidly regaining his stamina and he could get around pretty well.

Greg, his physical therapist, and Dr. Jan, his rehab doctor had met with him just last week. They weren't sure how much better he would get. It looked like the leg was as healed as it could be. He might see some minor improvement but from their point of view inpatient hospitalization was neither necessary nor helpful at this point.

The wound in his leg had shrunk slowly over the summer. He didn't notice any significant improvement from day to day. Then Alex or one of the other nurses would remind him how bad it had been at the outset and he'd think "yeah, it's really getting better." The smaller divot had disappeared into a clump of scar tissue. Scar tissue now covered most of the area.

The dressing change was no longer so extensive or difficult. He could do it himself at home, or so they told him.

Home. He should be excited. He could be going home soon, going back to his life. Or what was left of his life now. That would not be football and probably not be the A crowd either. But it would be Dan, his best friend. There were other friends. There was home itself. It would be nice.

But where would that leave Nikki? He couldn't leave her alone in this place. He had only managed to keep his sanity because of her. He remembered how he felt in those early days; the physical pain, the anxiety, the guilt. He had gotten through it all because of her. It felt unfair to desert her now.

Not that there was much he could do about it. This was the same medical bureaucracy that had declared Nikki a boy based on one DNA test fifteen years ago and tried to shove her into that same hole ever since. What chance did he have against it? It would declare him healthy and he'd been given his papers and shooed out the door, leaving Nikki to suffer alone.

He liked to pretend that he would come back and visit regularly, but he had to be realistic. It was hard enough for his parents to make it up to see him between work and everything else. How often would they be able to drive him up to see her?

There was only one way for him to stay, and that was to not be healthy. He had an idea about that, but it scared him more than he cared to think.

He could touch his wound. Just unwrap it in the middle of the night and touch it with his bare hands, just enough to infect it. An infection would keep him in the hospital and at Nikki's side.

It was crazy. He knew that. But it made it's own crazy sort of sense. Just get a minor complication, enough to stay a few more weeks, to see Nikki through this.

Then again, you didn't get to choose whether a complication was minor or not. He might get one of those rare infections and be in isolation, where he wouldn't be allowed to see Nikki anyway.

He even went as far as toying with the top of ace wrap that held the dressing in place. He couldn't bring himself to do more than that though.

He had a few more days, maybe even a week, to think about it. He decided to think his plan over in the cold light of day before doing anything. It was after two am before he finally managed to get some sleep.

#

Jason arrived for physical therapy the next day to find a new partner, Nikki. Her IV had been capped off except when she was getting antibiotics. She was dressed in hospital scrub pants and a baby-blue short-sleeved T-shirt with the University of Iowa logo splashed across the front. "Andrea brought it in for me," Nikki said, "it was her daughter's but she's outgrown it."

Jason found it oddly out of character for Andrea "McBitch" to have brought Nikki a present, let alone a girl's T-shirt. Maybe she felt bad for all the shots she had forced on Nikki?

Nikki's presence in physical therapy was explained by Greg. "Six weeks in a wheelchair waiting for that graft to heal is a long time to be immobile. We need to build Nikki's endurance up. I hear you two are friends so I want you to do some laps together." He said.

So they did. It was weird having Nikki walking beside him instead of being in her wheelchair.

They did four laps before Nikki started to wince and complain that she was sore "down there". Greg had her sit out while Jason did four more laps. Then they did another four together.

It was nice and it gave them some time to talk.

#

That afternoon Alex came into his room and sat down. Jason looked at him and realized that whatever was coming was serious. He sat his iPad down and waited.

"I've had a long talk with Greg," Alex began, toying with one of Jason's crutches nervously. "He thinks you are holding back in therapy."

Jason stiffened. It was true, he had to admit. At first he had been fighting, each session was like a football practice. He gave a hundred and ten percent. Lately though he had been coasting more and more.

"I told him I thought I knew what was

going on and said I'd have a talk with you." Alex said.

"Okay," Jason said slowly, pretty sure that Alex had no clue what was going on.

Alex laid his chin on the crutch and regarded Jason thoughtfully. Quietly he said, "You know you can't save her like this."

Jason stared at him in shock. If Alex had guessed that much, did he know that Jason had thought about giving himself an infection on purpose? He blushed heavily and looked down.

"I can see what's going on," Alex persisted, "And I understand. Heck, your loyalty to Bobby and her, it's your best trait, bro. I respect that about you."

Jason was a long time in answering. "They don't understand," he said slowly, then he flushed with anger, "They don't understand! Just because they did some test years ago they think they know Nikki. None of those doctors have taken the time to get to know the real her. If they did they would understand how much they are hurting her! But nobody seems to understand."

"Hey!" Alex said sounding hurt, "some of us understand, okay? There's a reason I don't work that side of the hall."

Jason looked at him in a stunned silence.

"I couldn't do the shots," Alex said quietly. Alex was revealing things that were way out of 'accepted topics' range, but Jason swore he'd never rat Alex out. "I couldn't force it on her."

"Andrea," Jason began fuming.

"Wait," Alex said with a warning finger, "Don't say another word. I know what you, Bobby and Nikki call her. And I'll admit she's pretty abrasive sometimes but she's a good nurse and she's my co-worker.

"Would a good nurse," Jason started but Alex interrupted him again.

"And," he said over Jason's comment, "there's a reason Dr. Beth Wilson is involved in this case."

That stunned Jason into silence.

"Dr. Beth Wilson is head of pediatric endocrinology." Alex explained, "She doesn't see just any patients. Do you really think Dr. Kinnick invited her down here? or Dr. Hausbender?" Alex stared at Jason. "One of the nurses lodged a complaint with the bio-ethics department. That's the only reason she even knew about Nikki's case."

Jason thought about Andrea's gruff mannerism and for the first time thought about what sort of pressure she might be under. Did the doctors know it was her that complained? He nodded to Alex, "I am sorry, I just thought," he said.

"I know," Alex said quickly. "Obviously, I am not supposed to be telling you any of this, and without knowing it, I can see what our actions might look like. What I am trying to tell you is that there are people helping Nikki, whether you are aware of it or not. Plus we've gotten lax, you two spend so much time together and it's good for both of you, so we let you. But Nikki won't be abandoned when you leave. We'll be there for her."

"Thanks a lot man," Jason said.

"Besides she won't be here long anymore either." Alex said. "Now that the graft has been removed, the wound will heal quickly. She'll be going home soon too."

"But Dr. Hausbender said something about trying again?" Jason asked.

"Think," Alex commanded. "They can't do that right away. They'll have to let the area heal and then schedule something. It took months to get this all set up. It will be next summer at the earliest and,"

"And the care conference will be before then," Jason said with a smile, "Beth will get her say and maybe Nikki's parent will tell him to go take a hike."

"We can only hope," Alex agreed, "plus Nikki's getting older too. She has more right to say what her own care should be. They can't decide for her for much longer."

"Awesome," Jason agreed.

Alex sighed and stood, "Now I am going to tell Greg you are going to give it your all from now on. And I am going to tell the wound nurse you'll pay more attention and learn to do the dressing change yourself, right?" He gave Jason a meaningful look.

"Yeah," Jason agreed.

"And this conversation didn't happen,

either." Alex said.

"Of course not," Jason agreed emphatically. As Alex started towards the door Jason called for him. He stopped. "Thanks for not having this conversation with me." Jason said with a grin.

"Anytime," Alex replied, "anytime."

#

"Well," Greg said, "This is it."

Jason stared down at the crutch on the exam table in front of him. It was oddly shaped, a single piece of metal with a handle and C-shaped "cup holder" for his arm. It was called a Canadian Crutch.

"The good news," Greg went on, "is that if you can master this, there is only one crutch. That leaves your left hand free to carry bags or whatever." He paused and sighed. "The bad news is that this is probably it for us. If we brace your knee anymore you lose mobility. If we don't,"

"It gives out," Jason said. "I know. Maybe someday," he added wistfully.

Greg patted him on the back. "Maybe someday," he agreed, "You're young, you might have some nerve healing yet. Heck for that matter you're young and they are making new discoveries every day."

"Screw it," Jason said sharply reaching for the crutch. Greg looked at him nervously until Jason added, "I mean screw someday. Coach used to say, people always say 'someday' but someday doesn't matter. What matters is today. Make the most of today and the somedays will take care of themselves."

Greg smiled, "wise words, man, wise words."

Jason stood while Greg adjusted the height of the handle to fit him. Then Greg walked him around the therapy room. "Keep your body upright," he said, "try walking with as normal of a gait as you can, don't lean on the crutch. It's there if your knee gives out. But try not to overuse it."

Jason did his best to follow Greg's advice. His knee still gave out on almost every step. One side of his leg remained numb and his movements were still choppy. But he was up and he was moving. No, he wouldn't be playing football this fall but he'd be walking the halls going to class like everyone else.

CHAPTER TWENTY

Chapter 20: The Care Conference

"HERE are your scripts," Alex said handing Jason a small stack of white papers. "There is one for prescription strength Ibuprofen, six hundred milligrams. You can fill it or take three over-the-counter pills, no more than every six hours, okay?"

Jason looked through the stack. There were a lot.

"The rest aren't for medications, they're for your medical supplies, gauze, sterile water, Acetic acid, everything you need for your dressing change."

"I didn't realize I need a prescription for those," Jason said.

"For your parent's insurance to pay, you do." Alex replied. "We've got a note for your school, outpatient rehab should count as your PE requirement. This booklet has all the important numbers, your doctors, our nurse's station in case you forget something, the wound nurse, etc."

Jason's mom held out a plastic bag filled with dressing supplies and Jason folded the papers and put them in. He placed his arms in the Canadian Crutch and heaved himself upright. It felt odd to be dressed in his street clothes again. His jeans hid the damage to his leg and catching sight of himself in the mirror he looked whole again. Except for the crutch, it would serve as a constant reminder of what the accident had cost him.

He looked at Alex and smiled. "I am going to miss you, bro." He said jokingly.

"Me too, bro, me too." Alex said.

Jason held out his hand. Alex eyed it for a second and then batted it aside. "After all we've been through?" He said with a laugh and swept Jason into a hug. Jason leaned into the hug, glad that Alex had chosen to express his affection this way instead of a simple handshake.

Alex let him go and hugged Jason's mother as well. "You guys all ready?" He said.

Jason looked at the clock on the wall and steeled himself for what came next. "No," he said, "There is something I got to do yet."

Alex glanced at the clock and gave Jason

a knowing look. He nodded. Jason's mom was looking at him uncertainly.

Alex said to her, "It will take about a half an hour or so. I am about due for a break anyway, why don't I walk you down to the cafeteria." Apparently appeased by Alex's obvious approval, she let herself be led away.

At the far end of the hall was the largest of the three conference rooms on the unit. It had it's own miniature waiting room of sorts, four chairs lined up along the opposite wall. Three of the four chairs were currently occupied. First was Larry Pagan in a tweed suit, his gut sticking out as he slumped back. He looked as harried and exhausted as ever. Next to him was his wife, Carol Pagan in a rumpled beige blouse and tan pants. She clutched a tan purse with tall wooden handles nervously. Next to her was a grim-faced Nikki, in hospital scrub bottoms and Andrea's baby blue T-shirt.

Jason sank into the final chair. He let go of the crutch and interlaced his hand with Nikki's. Her mom looked down at their hands and then away without commenting.

"So you got your walking papers?" Nikki said without meeting his gaze.

"Yup." Jason replied.

Through the half open door he could see Andrea sitting at the table in the conference room writing on a chart. Apparently she was putting the last few minutes before the conference to use catching up on her charting.

Dr. Kinnick was already in the room, looking at a magazine and periodically scowling around the room. Several other doctors or medical professionals that Jason did not know were in the room ranged around the table.

"So when are you leaving?" Nikki asked quietly.

"After this," he said with an air of determination.

"They won't let you in, you know." She replied.

"I know," He agreed. "But you'll know I am out here the whole time." He paused and added, "for you."

She squeezed his hand. "Thanks," she said. She looked at him and smiled.

Dr. Beth Wilson swept down the hall followed by a veritable entourage of people. "Are you ready?" She asked Nikki as she swept passed.

Nikki let go of Jason's hand and nodded. She rose and followed her parents into the room.

The entourage, Jason knew from what Nikki had told him earlier, included a fair number of people on the Bio-ethics committee. There would be doctors, a couple of managers and one of the hospital's legal team.

As they got settled into their seats, Andrea rose and came to shut the door. She gave Jason a sharp look. He met the gaze evenly. He was starting to judge Andrea and her looks differently since his conversation with

Alex and the gift of the shirt. He saw it not as disapproval but as a challenge. It was like when coach scowled at someone in practice. So he met her gaze and showed her he was strong enough to stand up for himself and for Nikki too. She gave him the slightest of nods and shut the door. He hoped he had read her right.

He sank back in the chair and for the next few minutes wished he'd thought to bring his iPad or something to do. But within five minutes he realized it didn't matter that they hadn't let him in, they were being so loud he couldn't help but hear.

Most of it was pretty predictable. Dr. Kinnick and Dr. Hausbender both insisted that "Nicholas" was male and that they had worked tirelessly to give him the guidance he needed to grow to accept himself as a male. Dr. Kinnick, in particular, managed to play off the obvious failures in this regard as someone else's fault. Nikki's parents or school had simply not understood or followed the program he had laid out correctly.

Dr. Beth Wilson was equally loud and insistent that the two men were working with a "dangerously outdated" concept of biology and gender. Regardless of DNA, Nikki was a girl and should be treated as such. She made a strong case, especially given the geneticist's findings that Nikki's body couldn't process testosterone correctly. Estrogen, and female puberty, were Nikki's best hope of normal maturity, Beth argued.

After almost thirty minutes of this, and more than one loud slap as someone hit the table in emphasis, a short silence fell. In the silence he heard Andrea's voice, "So Nikki, what do you think?"

There was another long pause and then Nikki's voice. "I think," she said "that this condition I have, and the fact that I don't have a clear answer to the one question that everyone else takes so much for granted, is hard and it sucks." There was a quiet hush of apologies and condolences but Nikki's voice rose above it. "But I think having a bunch of experts arguing over who I am and what it means to be me, isn't helping!"

"I am sorry, Beth," she went on, "I like you, I really do. But I am sick and tired of a bunch of doctors telling me how to live my life and who I should be. I don't want to stop seeing them and run straight into a different set of doctors with a different set of expectations. I feel like you've all had your chance. Now it's my turn."

"Of course, I understand," Beth said.

"I want to go home and just be myself for awhile. Maybe I will come back and start estrogen to be a girl, or maybe I will decide to be a boy after all, but it will be my decision." She said.

There was a murmur around the room.

"And you two, mom, dad," she said, "No more program, no more rules. And no more lies. I am want to go to school this year as Nikki."

"As a girl?" Her mother asked hesitantly.

"As myself," Nikki replied, "When they ask me, are you a boy or a girl? I am going to say, you know what? I don't know. Nobody does. I've been to the top doctors all over and nobody really knows. Maybe the kids can understand that, or maybe not. But it's the truth."

There was a long pause and then a voice that Jason couldn't recognize said, "Well, she's fifteen, she'll be sixteen soon and she's stated her wishes in a clear and reasonable manner. I think that's about it." He would learn later that had been the hospital's lawyer talking.

Clearly, it was the final word and moments later the table broke into a half dozen low buzzing conversations that Jason couldn't follow. It didn't really matter, Nikki had won.

Jason's mother returned while he was still sitting outside the conference room. She had a coffee cup in one hand and she sat down beside him. "How's it going?"

Before he could answer the door opened and Dr. Kinnick swept out, followed by Dr. Hausbender, Dr. Beth Wilson and her entire entourage. Last came Nikki and her family followed by Andrea. When Nikki caught sight of Jason she broke into a huge grin.

"I did it, Jason!" She said. "No program, no extra rules, no shots or surgery, nothing."

He smiled back at her. "That's great." He said.

"You seem really happy," Jason's mom said. Jason looked at her and realized he had only shared a fraction of Nikki's case with her. They would have to have a long talk on the way home before she would understand.

Nikki nodded. Her father was looking more uncertain, like he didn't know what to think. Her mother looked relieved. In fact she looked calmer than Jason had ever seen her.

"We just want what's best for our child," Nikki's mother said.

"Of course," Jason's mom agreed, confused.

To break what was likely to become an increasingly awkward conversation Jason said, "Nikki, mom and I are going to have to get going but could you walk part of the way with us? I want to say good-bye."

"Uh-huh" she agreed and to her parents she said, "Ill be right back, kay?"

She walked them all the way to front entrance. In the elevator Jason asked, "So how much longer do you think you'll have to stay?"

"Not long," she replied, "Just a couple of days or so. Now that every thing's over, it's almost ridiculous how little the wound is. It's like that whole part of the summer was just a bad dream and now I am waking up."

"Waking up to a whole new life," Jason said with a smile.

At the front entrance they stood

awkwardly, neither one knowing how to start. "I am glad you don't have to stay much longer either," He said.

"Yeah, it won't be the same without you." She replied. She blushed and looked down, "You know, when this summer began I never thought," she looked away across the lounge, "I never thought I would meet friends in a place like this. But I did. Two of them."

"One of them even survived," Jason joked. Then he stopped himself appalled and afraid. But Nikki just broke out giggling and fell against him. She wrapped her arms around his chest and hugged him tight.

"I don't think I could have made it without you." She said. "No I take that back, I know I wouldn't have made it. You saved my life, Jason Rembrandt. And I thank you."

He shrugged it off. "You saved my life too. I would have never been able manage, especially not those first few days. Thank you." He kissed her lightly on the forehead and hugged her back.

As they broke their hug he thought he caught a glimmer of tears in Nikki's eyes, but she was smiling and her face glowed. With a final good-bye he turned away and followed his mom out into the street and across the parking garage.

#

Jason hitched his bag up on his left shoulder. It felt awkward but he figured he'd eventually get used to it. It was easier than trying to carry anything on his right side, with the crutch and bad leg. He shifted his weight and looked back.

"Are you going to be okay?" His mom asked from the driver's side of her car.

"Yes," He replied testily and shooed her on her way.

As she drove off he turned back and regarded the school again. He began his slow shuffling gait up the parking lot and towards the main entrance.

"Awesome buddy," Dan called and ran over. He gave Jason a slap on the shoulder, which nearly caused his leg to buckle under him. "Seniors, man!" Dan said, "Can you freaking believe it? One more year and we are through with this place for good!"

Dan started up towards the entrance. A few steps ahead he looked back. "I'm coming," Jason said quickly. "I'm just slower than I used to be."

"It's okay bro," Dan said coming back to his side, "I just forgot. It's weird you know, you missed like the whole summer in that freaking hospital."

"Yeah," Jason agreed, though to himself he thought, summer? No, I have had a whole lifetime since last spring.

Brittany passed by the entrance in front of him. She gave him an awkward wave and a helpless shrug as Jeydon walked up and ushered her inside. Dan looked at Jason nervously as he watched them enter the school and disappear.

He looked at Dan and said, "It's okay." It was too. It felt like so long ago. He had changed so much in the last couple of months that it was almost surreal to realize how little everyone else had changed.

Inside the building a few of the football players came up to him and shook his hand or patted his back, congratulating him on his return. Then they would glance down at his leg nervously and he would wonder if their support was genuine or if it was show. He'd know in a few days, if they stuck by him or drifted off. That didn't matter either.

Last year he had strode these halls like a champion. This year he shuffled painfully, leaning on his one crutch and having to stop every few steps to readjust the bag that kept wanting to slide off his left shoulder.

But he didn't feel defeated. Last year he looked up and down these halls and saw the popular kids, his crowd. He saw the spazes, he saw band geeks, the math nerds, the bullies and the bullied.

Now he saw a skinny emo kid with a black stocking cap pulled down to his ears and he thought of Bobby. Would Bobby fit in at this high school? No. Was Bobby someone worth knowing? Heck, yes.

Maybe the emo kid had an awesome online profile and had earned every achievement in Halo, just like Bobby. Maybe the scruffy kid that everyone called a homo was like Nikki, unsure if he should be a boy or a girl. Maybe the heavy set girl with the short blond hair had read a million books and could discuss deep philosophical issues, like Nikki. Jason didn't know. He was determined to find out. Before the time the year was out he was determined to give each and every kid at school a chance; a chance to show him something other than a jock, a geek, a cheerleader, a spaz.

CHAPTER TWENTY-ONE

epilogue

WHO is my hero?
By Jason Rembrandt
For Mrs. Wheeler
Senior English

When we think of heroes we think of people who do things. We think of policemen who see what might be a car tipped over in a ditch and go check it out. We think of the EMT's who use the jaws of life to remove an injured boy from that car. We think of the life flight nurses, the trauma surgeons and all the people that struggle through the night to save that boy's life.

I met those sort of heroes this summer, though I barely remember most of them. I wish I could remember them all so I could go thank them, but I can't. I could pick any one of them for this essay, but I am not going to.

You see while lying in the hospital with the mangled remains of my leg in front of me I met a different kind of hero. I met people who are not heroes for what they do, but simply for being there.

I met a nurse who did incredible things. But the moments I will always remember were the ones where he sat quietly in a chair and listened while a whiny selfish little teenager actually complained because he had been given a second chance at life, because the life he had been given wasn't the perfect life he wanted.

And I met the bravest girl I have ever known. I know she was brave not because she ran into a burning building or something. She was brave because she cared. She cared despite the fact that she was going through her own private suffering. She cared despite the fact that many of the people she cared about were dying of cancer. Until our friend Bobby died I had no idea just how much bravery it took to watch someone suffer, knowing you couldn't help them, and not look away.

Because she never turned away from any one's suffering, I call this girl a hero; my hero.

#

Jason let the car coast into the parking

lot. He pulled the handbrake, put it in park and then shut the engine off. This was the place.

He got out, thinking about how much trouble he was likely to get into tonight. Oh well, either mom and dad would understand or they wouldn't. He had to do this.

But still, they had just gotten the hand brake installed so he could drive again. They had just given him permission to drive to school for the first time. And what did he do?

He ditched. For the first time ever, he ditched school.

"To go to another school?" Dan had said with a sigh, "Bro, we got to talk..."

Jason didn't care. He didn't care what his parent's thought or did to him when he got home. He didn't care what Dan or anyone at his school thought. Nikki wanted him here today, so he was here.

He looked at his watch. He had taken to wearing it on his left. Already that was starting to feel normal. It was almost time. He had to hurry. He pocketed his car keys, pulled his crutch out of the back seat and started towards the entrance.

It took only a few minutes to check in at the main office and find out where he was supposed to be going. He was running late and classes were in session. He shuffled down empty halls until he found the room he was looking for.

The entire class turned his direction as he opened the door. The teacher looked up and gave him a quizzical look. He saw a familiar hand go up at the front of the class. Nikki gestured at the teacher. The teacher shrugged and pointed towards a seat at the rear of the class. She turned and gave him a wave and a smile. She had told him on the phone that she had cleared it with the teacher and the school. The other students were all giving him curious glances.

The teacher cleared his throat. "Well, now that our guest has arrived," He said, "We have one last presentation for today. Those of you who have not completed your science presentations, we will do the rest next week starting on Tuesday. Now, Nikki?"

Nikki rose and went to the front of the class. She was wearing a lavender top and blue jeans. Her hair was longer. She stopped and pulled it together into a bun and then stuck a pencil through it to hold it in place. She had told Jason on the phone that despite her claim that she was done with experts she had seen Beth again. She found out through her reading that estrogen came in pills, not shots and immediately signed up. It would take months for breasts to grow but already with her hair longer she looked far more like a girl than a boy.

"Hello," She said as she got to the front of the class, "I'm Nikki Pagan, as you all know and my science presentation is going to be about sexual differentiation," There was a nervous titter at the word sexual. Nikki ignored it. She was typing on the teacher's computer as she spoke and a screen lit up behind her. She started a slide show and then she started into her presentation.

The first part of the presentation was about X and Y chromosomes and how the egg and the sperm meet and create either an XY male or an XX female. The presentation was way beyond the level of most of the students in the room and their eyes were slowly gazing over.

Then Nikki started talking about how in rare cases two sperm could enter the egg at the same time, resulting in an XXY intersex person. "It's called Klinefelter's disease," she said, "And that was the first diagnosis they gave me."

You could have heard a pin drop in the room over the next several seconds. Every eye was open and alert, fixed on the front of the room. "It was the wrong diagnosis." She said, looking at the teacher, "Moving on..."

And so it went. Nikki was coming out to her classmates in her own indirect way. She would start talking about a geneticist or doctor who made some discovery about intersex disorders. Just as the science was losing the kids she'd mention that she'd seen that guy. She talked about androgen insensitivity, about XY males that developed as females because their bodies didn't react to male hormones and then she said, "I don't have that either but it's about as close as the textbooks come. I don't react properly to testosterone."

By the end of her presentation she had laid it all out on the table, well almost all.

"So," one of the students asked after the presentation, "about your..." he trailed off with a vague gesture towards his crotch.

"My genitals?" She asked with one eyebrow arched.

He nodded.

"They are every bit as private as anyone else's."

The teacher coughed nervously, "Of course," he said. "Any other questions?" There were none. She had given them a lot to digest as it was. "Thank you, Nikki," he concluded, "That was a very good presentation of a very difficult subject." She beamed.

The final bell rang moments later and the students began to shuffle out of the room. Jason sat back in his chair and waited until most of them were gone and Nikki had gathered her books and was standing before him.

"That was really a great speech." He said, "well worth the drive."

"I am so glad you came," She said, "I was so nervous. I needed the moral support."

"Why?" He asked, "You did a great job." He stood and said, "So now what?" He followed her out into the hallway. A few students studied them curiously, but most of the other students were intent on getting home.

"Well," Nikki said, "first we are going to

see Alexis."

A sharp vision of a cemetery shot through Jason's head. He wasn't sure he was up to that. He gulped.

She must have caught his look. She laughed, "It's okay." She said, "She made it. Complete remission. Her hair is even growing back already."

He grinned. "Awesome."

"They don't all die you know." She said and she poked him playfully, "dork. Anyway I told her we'd stop by. Her mom wants us to stay for supper."

As they started down the hall he slid his left hand into hers. "You know, even when life isn't perfect it can be pretty good sometimes." He said.

"You're a wise man, Jason, a wise man." She replied.

CHAPTER TWENTY-TWO

About the Author

I hope you've enjoyed the story. If you have please leave a review on whatever site you purchased it. Or Goodreads. Honest reviews are the greatest gift you can give an author.

Rachel's Goodreads page can be found here:

https://www.goodreads.com/author/show/5376294.Rachel_Eliason

Rachel's writing explores diverse social topics and characters. She takes on LGBT issues and coming of age in her YA novels. Her writing has been described as engaging and thought provoking by critics and fans.

She also writes science fiction and fantasy under her initials R. J. Eliason. Her writing can be found wherever books are sold online.

Sign up for Rachel's newsletter here:
http://eepurl.com/cJAWX1

The End

www.ingramcontent.com/pod-product-compliance
Lightning Source LLC
Chambersburg PA
CBHW061613170626
46811CB00001B/421

* 9 7 8 0 9 8 8 5 7 3 0 2 4 *